I Never Did Tell You Did I?

(Unsent Letters)

Also by Susan Smith Nash:

Poetry and Fiction

Grammar of the Margin Road

My Love is Apocalypse and Rhinestone

Liquid Babylon

A Veil in the Sand

A Paleontologist's Notebook

Channel-Surfing the Apocalypse

Catfishes and Jackals

Doomsday Belly

To the Uzbekistani Soldier Who Would Not Save My Life

Blood and Oil

Translations

Tatapyípe: Junto al Fuego (Susy Delgado)

First Light: An Anthology of Paraguayan Women Writers

Ayvu Membire: Offspring of the Distant Word (Susy Delgado)

Cultural Studies

Dealing With Date Rape: True Stories from Survivors

I Never Did Tell You Did I?
(Unsent Letters)

Susan Smith Nash

Avec Books
Penngrove
2003

Grateful acknowledgment to the editors and translators of some of these letters, which first appeared in slightly different form in: *Portret Nemirne Americanke, Vodnikova Zalozba,* Ljubljana, Slovenia and *Sodobnost,* Ljubljana, Slovenia.

First Edition

ISBN:1-880713-32-2

Library of Congress
Control Number: 2003108333

Cover design by Colleen Barclay

Avec Books
P. O. Box 1059
Penngrove, CA 94951

November 28
Suthton, Vermont

Hi Tek —

Hey, I made it to Vermont! I flew in to Manchester, New Hampshire, then rented a car and made the three-hour drive across New Hampshire and up through the mountains of central Vermont — and now I'm in Suthton, just south of Montpelier, where you bought me the cute hand-beaded purse you gave me for my birthday last April.

Our lives have reversed themselves. You've got what I'd like to have — a nice house, a good situation with your kids, intellectual freedom — and I've got what you want — a job interview at a small, exclusive university in Vermont.

Maybe it's just what I need. I hope so. As you know, I've been having a hard time of it lately. The oil industry continues to implode. As a geologist, I have diversified into other things, but my heart's not really in it. One has to survive, though, right? I don't know why I've been so edgy and restless — I just feel I'm on the verge of something both terrible and wonderful, and I'm nervous about it.

Isn't it ironic, if you think about it? You travel from Oklahoma to Vermont at least three times per year, and I haven't been here for any length of time since I was a teenager and we spent all summer at the cabin. I'll never forget the argument Mom and Dad had when trying to resolve their differences over the plan. And yet, I've been the one who has claimed to hate Vermont — I've claimed to hate the smell of musty basements and the feeling of being lost in a forest that has no name and no way out. I always preferred to think of myself as a geologist — primarily petroleum, but also involved in minerals exploration. The very idea of the profession always gave me a sense of freedom.

Vermont never did that. Just think — there's the family cemetery — hidden in a corner of a remote scrap of forest, surrounded by a rusted iron fence, wild and treelike rose bushes twisted around the gates, and the fading tombstones themselves demonstrating how many women died in childbirth, and how many children died before the age of five.

I used to tell you that the bats that lived in the roof of our summer cabin were spirits from the cemetery coming to search for a living body to inhabit. You believed me, which was convenient — I had the upstairs bedroom, and it was large and comfortable. I didn't want a little sister sharing it with me. Unfortunately, on dark, misty nights when the rain hit the galvanized tin roof and the roar of the stream kept me awake, I would hear hushed voices and the sound of a little girl crying. I never told anyone.

And now I'm sitting in a cold room in an incredibly charming "bed and breakfast" establishment. It's a place you would love — an old Victorian mansion that has been renovated with antiques. The scent of cinnamon and pine pervades each of the three stories, and there is an atmosphere of quaint elegance.

There is also no telephone in my room. No television, Internet connection, no videocassette player, no DVD, no CD player. Nothing. Just a pile of magazines — *Vermont Life* and *Antiques in America.*

I'm looking out the window at the postcard-perfect scene outside. It's still snowing and there are icy spots on the road, but it's not bad. I'm glad, because to tell the truth, I was terrified of driving in a blinding snowstorm.

Plus, I can get out and drive to Montpelier. It's too quiet. Maybe there's some action there in the "big town" (population 12,000 even though it is the state capital). It's only 8:30 p.m.. Maybe I'll eat dinner there, drink a cappuccino, buy gifts, have my fortune told. Anything. I'm starting to think too much.

There is nothing more dangerous than introspection.

Love,
Susan

December 2
Suthton, Vermont

Hi Tek,

I finished up my interviews at Westhorpe University. It's a great place and I hope they offer me the position. It will be a change. I'll be letting geology go for good. Am I ready for it? I have no choice. At any rate, it's a final step.

I have a feeling they might offer me the job. However, I won't know until they interview three more people. They'll let me know around December 20. The people are great, and to be honest, it had a wonderful "coming home" feel to it all — perhaps that's because they are Vermonters and we are, in essence, "ethnic Vermonters." I know that sounds strange, but there really are social and cultural differences throughout the US. Vermonters are liberal in politics, conservative with finances, and have very dry senses of humor. They also appreciate the outdoors, like to pick berries in the summer, grow gardens, knit sweaters and socks, go trout fishing, hunt partridge, deer, and moose, set traps for raccoons in the garden, chop wood for the winter woodpile and shovel snow.

Chop wood? Shovel snow? I'm not feeling such an ethnic affinity any more.

On the last day, I attended a presentation by a sociology professor from a nearby university in Montpelier. It was fascinating, although uncomfortable. She's sort of the archetypal liberal professor, decked out in clogs and handwoven skirt / tunic attire. She cut quite the odd figure, since Westhorpe is a military academy, and the professors wear uniforms. She read a paper: "A Lacanian Interpretation of Westhorpe University Students," and described how the Westhorpe cadets fetishize torture rituals (called hazing) and other rites of passage because they are attempting to both mask and intensify the homoerotic worship of phallic authority. According to her, the goal of all these rituals is the secret spilling of body fluids while in pain. The best body fluid is blood, but urine and sweat are okay. Semen is problematic.

As she read her paper, I kept glancing at the faculty. I wanted to see their reaction. They were surprisingly calm about it, even as she got into the lurid details of why and how the torture rituals are kept secret and the body fluids are placed in hierarchies. The worst moment was when she explained why semen is problematic — it is problematic because it is associated with the female cadets whom, she claimed are called "buckets." The provost turned red, and some of the faculty squirmed in their seats.

Of course, I'm used to this sort of talk, and I'm used to the scandalizing language used in sociology of gender articles. But — this was completely different. Keep in mind that these are mainly engineering and mathematics professors who tend to take the vocabulary literally, rather than as the extended metaphor that it really is. She never mentioned whether or not there is a basic training or boot camp element. It sounded to me as though individuals had decided to make a kind of unsupervised "recruit training" event. Everyone wants to be the DI (drill instructor), I guess. Sounds dangerous, if what she said was true.

During the question-and-answer time, there were a few feeble protests that what she presented was, at best, a sensation-seeking caricature of reality, and that her thesis seemed exaggerated. Mainly, though, there were polite comments about how valuable it was to be introduced to the theories of Lacan in such an accessible way. She would respond by reading more passages — lurid passages about blood hierarchies and when the rituals took place, and how measuring body fluid spillage took on a scatological mixture of the sacred and the profane.

As she went on and on, I kept wondering how the cadets spilled blood. Did they cut themselves accidentally while crawling through passageways in the dark? Was it their blood? Did it have to be human blood? Could they simply go on a hunt — fox, deer, or dog — then dip something in the blood?

I was afraid to ask.

Finally, it was over (to my regret), and the director of the search committee drove me back to the Suthton Inn. He asked me how much I'm making in my current position, and then he commented that he hoped that the afternoon lecture didn't give me a bad impression of Westhorpe. I told him that I enjoyed it because any time anyone uses Lacan's theories and applies them to a real-life situation, the results are as entertaining as a tabloid newspaper.

Love,
Susan

ON MAD COW DISEASE AND IMPRESSIONS OF EUROPE

December 11
Norman, Oklahoma

Dear Todd,

Hey, thanks for the Mad Cow animation that you sent me in your last e-mail.

I'll be at your birthday party on Saturday. Please don't make Mad Cow jokes at my expense — especially if Mom and Dad are within earshot. You know how they worry. I don't have mad cow disease! I did not eat tainted meat while I was in London. Further, although I am eccentric, I am not "mad" and although female, I am not a cow. At least I'm not admitting to it. For your information, I did not eat any meat. At least I don't remember eating meat. I think I stuck to scones, espresso, followed by warm beer guzzled at a pub near Paddington Station. Plus, I was only in London for a day as I made my way back from the Caspian region.

And, by the way, I don't think that mad cow disease is a laughing matter, even though the animation you sent me — the cow laughing hysterically while its brain is being fried during electric shock treatment at a psychiatric hospital — is pretty funny.

While I was in London, two things occurred to me about mad cow disease. First, it didn't seem all that surprising that the British would feed cow bones to their cows as a dietary supplement. They probably considered it okay, but only if the cows were Egyptian, Jamaican, Nigerian, or (of course) Pakistani. That's precisely what the British have been doing for three centuries. Mad cow disease seems to be the perfect metaphor for the logical consequence of colonialism, doesn't it?

The other thing that occurred to me is that while Western Europeans seem to be comfortable with the commercial and travel benefits of a "borderless Europe" and the Euro, psychologically there is a deep mistrust of their neighbors. Actually, who can blame them? Just take a look at their history, both distant and recent.

So, mad cow disease becomes a convenient pretext for erecting new barriers, new borders. The fear of contamination and infection is reasonable and justified. However, it makes me wonder if, on some deep level, Western Europeans view people of non-Western European origins as somehow capable of contaminating them or infecting them? Western Europe doesn't seem to enjoy thinking of itself as a great melting pot. In fact, the people seem to go to great lengths to make certain that there are clear differences between people of various nationalities, and there is a clear hierarchy. The "real" or the "authentic" Europeans seem to have a better time of it than the "guests."

I know you say this happens here in the US, but I just don't think it's really the same. Are we afraid of being contaminated or infected by our neighbors? Do we think of our neighbors as bringing disease into our nation? Upon reflection, I suppose the answer to those questions is "yes." Think of the Mexicans. We allow them in (illegally, we claim), and they are expected to wash dishes in restaurants, cut grass, paint houses, and work on road crews. There is also the idea that they can contaminate communities by bringing in black-tar heroin from Mexico, and forming violent gangs. And, when the Haitian immigrants first began to come into Florida, a large percentage were sent back because they carried the AIDS virus.

So, we're not so different in our attitudes, but I think that the Western Europeans damage the world with their legacy of colonialism. It is an attitude of automatic entitlement, and of viewing the rest of the world as a place that one can go and live like a prince, and once one has had one's fill of novelty, one can go back home.

Of course, if one is an American, it is very hard to cast stones. I suppose the world considers us dull-minded, spoiled, rich and arrogant bullies.

I'll never forget when Mother and Dad gave me a graduation present for finishing high school with perfect marks. Do you remember? They gave me a round-trip ticket and $300 to fly to Bolivia and visit my friend, Violeta, who had been an exchange student here in Oklahoma the year before. How enlightened they were! It didn't seem to bother them at all that their 18-year-old daughter was flying alone to Santa Cruz, Bolivia. And this was before fax machines, before e-mail, before there were even telephones in much of Bolivia. It was wonderful! Little did anyone realize that Violeta and her family did not know I was coming, and that my arrival was a complete shock. But, Violeta and her family were nice about it. They let me stay with them.

Once there, I was glad I had spent so much time studying Spanish. I was absolutely fascinated by Bolivia. I observed that the Americans who worked for oil companies had great lives. They went from stressful and uncomfortable lives as low-level functionaries in big, dirty American cities to overlords of their fiefdoms with expansive villas in Bolivian towns where they had their own swimming pools, cooks, chauffeurs, maids, and invitations to the most exclusive soirees and events.

That is when I decided that I wanted to live in Bolivia. I wanted to go back there and live like a queen. It never happened, but the image of that life motivated me to study and to be curious about life outside the US.

And that brings me back to the question of your birthday and the fantasy life of your eight-year-old son.

Why not encourage him to dream? What's wrong with having fantasies of wearing crowns, jewel-bedecked necklaces, and long, shiny robes? In my opinion, everyone should be allowed to dream, regardless of whether or not it seems "appropriate" to one's station in life, nationality, or gender.

After this letter, I don't expect to be invited to your birthday party. So, I'll just say in advance, "So what! I don't care! I didn't want to go anyway!"

Now that I've dealt (in advance) with the sting of rejection, I'll wish you again, a VERY HAPPY BIRTHDAY.

Love,
Susan

ON WHY I DON'T LIKE TAKING THE PLACE OF YOUR ANTIDEPRESSANT MEDICATION

December 13
Norman, Oklahoma

Rialdi,

Thanks for getting together for lunch yesterday — and, thanks for letting me be so honest with you about my feelings.

Actually, it's easier to run away (emotionally or physically), but I suppose it's worthwhile to make an honest assessment of the situation and to articulate my thoughts and feelings. I don't really want to write this letter, but I think that it's the least I can do. You deserve to know what's on my mind. On the other hand, to write this seems pretty cruel, and I'd rather just let everything slide. I just don't know!

For almost two years, we've seen each other intermittently — it seems to go pretty well for awhile, and then I "disappear." At least that is how you describe it. And I agree, at least that is what it looks like on the surface.

But it all starts and ends with the question: "Why is it that when you're with me you feel good about yourself? And, why is it that when I'm with you I feel so BAD?"

Your sister who lives in England said that perhaps the reason a relationship between the two of us has never worked out is because you're "sorted out" and sometimes it's not easy to be around a person who is completely "sorted out."

You then explained to me (as though I were some sort of idiot) that "sorted out" is a British term, and that she has lived so long in England that she has become British. And, besides, your mother was a British citizen who was raised in China by governesses and servants because her father was the economic attaché (or something along those lines) at the British Embassy in Peking (or somewhere). You're very proud of that aristocratic lineage. I don't blame you. I think it partially explains why you enjoy working with local heads of state (Oklahoma governors, etc.).

That's nice. Now that we've established that you are firmly five or ten rungs of the ladder above me, and that I have no hope of ever aspiring to your lofty perch, we can go on.

I suppose the underlying assumption is that you think I'm not "sorted out" — and, in fact you said that you questioned yourself deeply, wondering if you were attracted to me because of some sort of "broken wing" syndrome — suggesting that I'm a bird with a broken wing and that you feel compelled to "rescue me" — out of noblesse oblige, I suppose. You always like to mention that I'm a geologist at a time when small and medium oil companies have all but disappeared. Not only are we talking about depletion of reserves here in Oklahoma, but also the fact that business conditions have changed, and the small companies just can't compete against the large ones.

Sharks eat minnows. They always have. They always will.

I may be a minnow, but I'm not a bird. And, for your information, I do not have a broken wing. But, I think you know that — and, my exaggerating the somewhat tragic aspects of my miserable, sordid, little failed life is simply a way to save face.

You claimed that you told your sister that even though you are indeed completely "sorted out," you have come to realize that something is missing. That missing element is love. By love, I think you mean a woman, a helpmate, a companion, a sounding board, a receptacle of all you have to give. Some people refer to that as a "bucket."

In theory, I wouldn't mind being your love-bucket. I do enjoy your conversation and your company, but after I'm with you, I feel as though a thousand birds have just picked the flesh from my bones.

Yesterday, I explained to you that after getting to know you, instead of admiring, loving, and accepting you, I'm simply riddled with envy and jealousy. How to you explain that? Hmm.

And, even though you are willing to accept me as a person who is not "sorted out" (but, as you conceded, "bright"), I just can't perform up to your expectations. I'm supposed to be falling all over myself to make big, blatant shows of affection and devotion. I'm supposed to be foaming at the mouth to have sex, etc.. You said you were disappointed that I didn't seem to be more delighted to see you when you came back from Hawaii.

But, the truth was, you were only gone a week! And I hate it that you keep wanting to make huge displays of emotion in public places — holding hands, chewing on my fingers, etc.. I grew up in this town, and this is a conservative society — what are you thinking?

You can have a lot of things in life through sheer force of will and intense desire. You generally get what you want.

I've made a mistake in trying to force myself to make a relationship work, and for thinking that just because you want me, you should have me. After all, you are my better, aren't you?

My mother always told me it was just as easy to fall in love with a rich man as a poor one, so why not choose the rich one?

Well, sadly enough, it has been my experience that love is more like *A Midsummer Night's Dream* — I fall in love with asses. (But they can be so cute!)

And, in the meantime, I still ask myself the question: "If, after being together, you feel great, fantastic, on top of the world, and I feel utterly wretched, what's going on?"

I'm a walking dose of Zoloft for you. Or, Paxil — whatever the most effective antidepressant medication on the market might be . . . .

This is a really cruel letter, and I don't think I should send it.

I'll just call you and tell you that I'm not feeling well tonight and can't get together. Then, I'll simply disappear again.

That is the most diplomatic approach, isn't it?

Just call me "Coward." It's better than "Love-Bucket."

Sending this anyway,
Susan

December 14
Norman, OK

Hey Tek:

Do you want to go to inspect the tank battery at Wanette? I'm taking off after lunch. It takes about an hour to get there. I got a call from Gordo, the pumper, who said it looked like one of the tanks is leaking. Anyway, I need to find out what's going on. I know the tanks are pretty old — and they're probably corroded, even though they're repainted each year. There are four tanks. They hold the oil for that unit. There's another tank battery on the other edge of the field.

This is pretty depressing. It will be expensive — just at a time we can't really afford to have any catastrophic maintenance items. Not only is the price of oil low, but production is down. We really need to go in and clean up some of the wells — a shot of acid, perhaps pull pipes. Some sort of reconditioning. It's hard to justify the expense, though.

It just reminds me, yet again, how difficult things are here in rural Oklahoma.

On the way back, I think I'll stop in at the Wanette Diner. They have a great pecan pie, and they get homemade Italian sausages from Krebs, near McAlester.

In a perfect world, being a petroleum geologist and part owner of a small oil field would be a great thing. One has to keep the field maintained, and there are various production problems to tend to, but there's not much actual day-to-day work. In an ideal situation, the royalty checks would keep rolling in, month after month — like rent. It would provide a nice living, if one had a bit of success, and then was careful.

If the tanks have a small, corroded spot, then perhaps we can repair them. We'll drain them, then weld a patch. If not, we'll have to replace the tanks with new ones. That will require us to get new permits, plus do an inspection to make sure that there has been no surface spill and that no soil or water has been contaminated. This makes me worried —

Leaky tanks. Corrosion. Slow oxidation, resulting eventually in catastrophic failure. Sounds like a metaphor for love, or the human condition.

I think I prefer growth metaphors, or those that have to do with new discoveries, fonts of new life.

We'll see.

Give me a call if you'd like to go. I hope you get this e-mail before I have to take off.

Love,
Susan

ON UZBEKISTAN, TRAVEL EXPERIENCES AND THE "OTHER" (SPEAKING OF WOMEN)

December 14
Norman, OK

D:

I haven't heard anything from Westhorpe. I'm starting to try to talk to Marshall about the move — if I get the offer. He seems to be pretty excited about it. He likes the idea of a military environment.

One thing that Westhorpe liked about my application was that I had international experience. They are wanting to get into training and they like that I've had my own business and have supported myself exclusively through doing various types of economic development work, as well as continuing to keep the doors open with my little import-export firm. I established it years ago as a way to provide a backup for my geology career.

They are particularly interested in Central Asia. I have not told them about when Marshall and I went to Uzbekistan.

It would be exciting to brag that I've been to Uzbekistan, but I'm generally too paranoid. I'm afraid if I share stories, people might think I'm a sympathizer of Islamic fundamentalists. Granted, that's not too likely, since I don't seem too overtly masochistic and my political sentiments tend toward the maudlin and theatrical, depending on the audience.

Sadly, I can't calm down enough to enjoy regaling people with stories of men in robes and tasseled hats, women in flowered headscarves and electric, neon silks selling dried fruits on street corners, and women in local *chai-hanas* (tearooms) who served up rather oily but steaming chai in little cut glass cups, with bits of lemon peel floating on the surface, and a dish of sugarcoated peanuts and raisins as an accompaniment. Tashkent is a very modern city in the Soviet manner, rebuilt after devastating earthquakes in the 1960s. It's dusty, and now the massive Soviet-block buildings are crumbling, but overall, Tashkent is a pleasant city. There are parks with clusters of trees, and the smell of smoke in the morning as people burn leaves. Nevertheless, traces of the old city remain, and one can see echoes of the famous Central Asian architecture, with the domes, calligraphy, and gorgeous turquoise tiles.

The women of Uzbekistan were an enigma to me, but I'm not able to puzzle out the significance of anything — at least not now. Thanks to current events, my friends know about Central Asia and the plight of the Afghan women, but their understanding is a caricature. What is life like for women in Central Asia? My friend Marina is of Russian descent. She has dark brown hair, a heart-shaped face, full lips, and a direct demeanor. Clearly, her life is difficult, not only because of the general economic collapse that accompanied the breakup of the Soviet Union, but also because she is of Russian descent, and thus automatically hated by Uzbeks who were second-class citizens in their own country, and oppressed by the Russians.

A trained microbiologist who studied in Moscow at a prestigious Institute, Marina specialized in sheep parasites. Now she's working with the World Bank to help small businesses develop markets and find investment in rural Uzbekistan. The other two Uzbek women I met were both married to Ilgar, a heart specialist, turned economic development specialist, also employed by the World Bank. Very bright, kind, resourceful, patient, with a good sense of humor, Ilgar seemed to me the kind of person who would be able to succeed no matter what the circumstances.

In his late thirties, Ilgar was a slender, wiry man with a round face, pleasant facial expressions. When he mentioned he had two wives, I was immediately intrigued. Why would either one of them put up with it? He explained that it wasn't really normal in Tashkent, although Islamic law allowed up to four wives. He just couldn't decide. He had married Gula, his first wife, after finishing medical school. He showed me a photograph of her. She was slender, elegant, with dark hair and a thin face. Then they had problems, separated, and he met Natyala. She was equally slender, with a rounded face and pleasant smile. Then, they started having problems, and he started to see Gula again. To complicate things, he had a child with each. Now he couldn't decide between the two of them. I thought this was refreshingly honest.

"There is no money for doctors. No money for scientists. We have to become businessmen." That is what Ilgar repeated over and over. Marina echoed the sentiments. I looked at the threadbare bazaars, the street vendors selling products culled from their own homes, intellectuals going from person to person trying to sell books and personal items, and I felt depressed. If "business" was the only option, where was the business? Who were the customers?

One brisk morning in November, Marina and Ilgar decided to take me to the bazaar, while Marshall slept in. We were staying in an apartment that had recently been remodeled, and had new bathroom, new kitchen appliances, but very little furniture. The furniture miraculously appeared after I paid the week's rent in cash. Apparently, thanks to a black market exchange rate that was 500% better than the "official" exchange rate, each $60 per night for a luxurious two-room apartment was the equivalent of a month's salary. It was still a great deal for me, though, since Americans were generally charged "foreigner" rates at the hotels, which were at least $200 per night. We drove to the bazaar, stopped at a little *chai-hana* and ordered tea and pastries.

As we ate the typical Uzbek bread, *nan,* fresh from the tandoor, and sipped the scalding tea, a man in a gray sweater, button-down shirt, and corduroy pants approached me. He was carrying books in French, German, and English. He was asking me if I were interested in purchasing them. Marina looked a bit disturbed — she mentioned to me that he was probably a professor selling off his library in order to buy bread. I didn't buy the books. Later, I felt a bit guilty, but what could I do? I could have given him money. I didn't. My lack of generosity and fellow feeling left something to be desired, but I just hated being targeted just because I looked like a "rich American." "Aren't all of you rich?" was the unspoken question.

It didn't seem to bother Marshall. He liked the fact that with a $20 bill, he could go via taxi virtually anywhere, go to a disco, and buy *shashlik,* pizza and drinks (beer, I later found out!), for himself and five or six Uzbek teenagers. He liked being a "rich American."

"I'm not rich," I said as often as I could. "We look rich in America, but we're not. We can get 30-year loans for our houses, 5-year loans for cars, credit cards for everyday stuff. We look rich. We're not." Then, back in my room, I would peel off a $20 bill from the fat wad of money (I brought in $3,400 in cash to cover all expenses, since no one would accept credit cards, and there were no ATMs), and give it to Marshall so he could go with Marina's son, Kostya, via taxi to the local restaurants and treat all the friends to *shashlik* (shish-kabob) that was, in US dollars, about 11 cents per skewer.

They were also drinking beer and vodka, and relieving their overfull bladders by peeing on construction equipment (in one case, the seat of an old Russian tractor). Then Marshall, Kostya, and friends would go to a disco where girls would flock around him. I saw a Polaroid picture he had taken one night — he's standing in a dark disco, glitter ball hanging from the ceiling, and he's got a cigarette in one hand, a beer in the other, and five Uzbek girls hanging around him. He appears to be in heaven. When Marshall showed that Polaroid picture to his buddies back at home, all his friends immediately wanted to go to Uzbekistan. At one point, Marshall had a group of a dozen 14-year-old males who wanted to spend all summer in Uzbekistan, I guess to laze around until two or three in the afternoon, eat *shashlik*, smoke and drink beer in discotheques all night long. Well. Who could blame them? In a way, I was happy to see Marshall out acting like a typical teenager.

At home, he spent entirely too much time in front of the computer, glued to video games, or simply watching the latest popular television show. That year, it was *South Park.* The year before, it had been *Beavis and Butthead,* and before that, *Ren and Stimpy, The Simpsons,* and *Rugrats.* Some of those had already been exported — Marshall and I watched German-language dubbed *Rugrats* from our hotel room in

Frankfurt as we connected from Uzbekistani Airways to an American Airlines flight from Frankfurt to Chicago. It was a sad transition back into the American commercial culture-drenched world.

My experience of Uzbekistan was entirely different. I became some sort of symbol of US economic aid programs. Either I was rich, or I had a lot of pull at the State Department. At least that was what people thought. I kept insisting that I was just Miss Nobody of the Next-to-Poorest State of the Union. Of course, no one believed me. It was assumed that I had good connections and that I could get funding for programs, just through my personal influence at home. When I realized it, I felt despairing and pessimistic. Of course, I completely masked my negativity with a smiling, cheerful, optimism. "Let's try eco-tourism! Historical tourism! Let's organize a trade mission!" These were some of my more boneheaded ideas. I mean, there is no doubt that Uzbekistan is fascinating and historical. After all, there is the fabled Samarqand and the Silk Road, the land of Tamerlaine (Timur, the Great), Bukhara, and the lovely Fergana Valley which borders Tajikistan (and a civil war raging there). The Fergana Valley was famed for its fruits and vegetables, and certainly the pomegranates, apples, pears, peaches, apricots, grapes, raisins, peanuts, almonds, pistachios, dates, tomatoes, cucumbers and melons. I tried all that I could. They were spectacular.

Now they say the Fergana Valley is horrendously dangerous.

Things change, don't they. Usually for the worse.

All best,
Susan

ON AMERICAN TOURISTS IN UZBEKISTAN: WHY OR WHY NOT A GOOD IDEA?

December 15
Norman, OK

D:

I got an e-mail from Westhorpe today which said they were still considering me, and that they would have a decision sometime within two weeks.

They mentioned Central Asia again. That made me think of all the crafts there.

The crafts of Uzbekistan are unique, with lavish embroidery and patterns that remind one of Aladdin or Persian stories that speak of Sufic ecstasy and a mind dreaming, flying in fact, on a magic carpet. My favorites were the hats, the robes, the embroidered scarves, earrings, lacquered boxes, and porcelains.

But who in their right mind can possibly expect a group of seniors (the largest cohort of international travelers, aside from students) to carry all their money in cash — thousands of dollars! — and to travel to places where the restrooms consist of a hole in the ground that is, as Marina put it, "not comfortable"? (By the way, she wasn't kidding. The smell was ghastly, even in the office buildings where the restroom situation was the same.) This is just not realistic. The food will frighten the cholesterol and fat-gram counting Americans, too. Imagine a skewer of *shashlik* that consists of sheep fat, sheep meat, sheep liver, sheep fat. Marshall loved it. I ate it and wondered how on earth everyone stayed so slim. Of course, they weren't hauling American dollars, and chances are they weren't eating three enormous meals per day.

An adventure traveler might like Uzbekistan until he or she came to realize that an Intourist mentality still reigned supreme. You stay in a bus, you listen to a tour guide, you take pictures only when indicated. Never, never, try to take a picture of the Metro (I tried and was stopped in mid-click by a policeman). Don't wander around alone. Don't go up into the mountains alone. Stay with the group. Conform and be herded like sheep. What kind of adventure tourist can tolerate that?

This morning, I contemplated wearing one of the Uzbek sequined hats, at least, to the office as a gesture of Halloween esprit de corps. That would not have been as bulky as the whole ensemble, with long coat, silk scarves, knife strapped on the side, and little harem slippers. I decided against it.

Later in the afternoon, I decided that my travels to Uzbekistan and other Islamic countries in the former Soviet Union had made me a target for extreme surveillance when my e-mail messages for the year 2001 mysteriously disappeared. I immediately suspected my Internet service provider.

"Help! You'll never guess what happened! All my e-mail from this year has been EATEN! Someone or something has stolen it from my computer! I'm being invaded!"

I downloaded the latest anti-virus update and ran scan after scan. Nothing.

Then I checked my hotmail account. There was a weird message from a guy with the same name, but different middle initial, as my ex-husband. Over the weekend, I had been idly entering in his name in a search engine (indulging in a bit of virtual stalking). I suppose I just wanted to torture myself with bad memories, as I was curious to see to what he might be up to out there in cyberspace. I didn't find anything on the real "ex" — just stuff on other guys with the same name. One was a health science professional in the southeast. He seemed decent. Why couldn't I have married him instead of his worthless namesake? Of course, I'm sure the ex thinks the same of me whenever he happens along someone with my name.

I was almost disappointed when I realized that my e-mail messages hadn't disappeared at all, but that they were simply on some other part of the hard drive. The computer still indicated the presence of more than 3,000 e-mail messages. They hadn't disappeared. They were simply in some strange nether region of my computer. That was inconvenient, but not sinister. Nevertheless, I felt a great sense of loss. What if there were a love letter in there amongst the messages I hadn't had a chance to read yet? Would I be cut off forever from the very possibility of contacting him?

Marina sent me an e-mail from Tashkent. She mentioned that times were very dangerous now, with war at their doorstep. It seemed entirely possible that rebels could invade; after all, while I was in Samarqand, we visited madrassahs and mosques.

"The Islamic church is very popular now," Ilgar had told me. "They offer homes and shelter to people who have lost everything. Their followers are very loyal."

As he spoke, I began wondering what his home life must be like, with two wives. Did they live in the same house? Apparently not. In fact, one still lived with her family. Did they have the same profession? Apparently not. One was a health professional. The other worked for the government. They were both delicate and slender. I felt like a big, blonde behemoth. Could they ever complain? What would happen to them if they did?

I thought of the times I had been to Baku, Azerbaijan, which jutted out into the Caspian Sea off the Absheron Peninsula. Illuminated by the fires that burned from natural gas seeps, the coastline was an eery shade of red and orange. Silhouetted against the sky was the famed Maiden's Tower, a circular tower of stone, minutes from the walled city of Old Baku. According to legend, a king, the Shirvan Shah, walled up his daughter after she threatened to run away and marry someone other than the Shirvan Shah's choice. She lived alone in the tower, but at night, she would let down her long hair, and her lover would climb in and visit her. It was the original Rapunzel tale, a fact that had astonished me. I had always thought of Rapunzel as being of Western European origin.

You could be a male Rapunzel. Do you like the idea? The ultimate tease...

Thinking of you,
Susan

ON KNIVES, UZBEKISTAN, AND THE PERSISTENCE OF ALADDIN

December 16
Norman, OK

D:

I was digging through my files on Uzbekistan, and wondering if they are worth keeping. Central Asia is a crazy place — fruit, knives, and great Silk Roads. It sounds romantic. In reality, it leads to extremely heavy luggage.

It also encompasses the Fergana Valley. It's a great fruit and vegetable-producing region. It also contains significant reserves of oil and gas. I would love to visit some drilling operations, or visit the fields. That's very much off-limits, though.

Marshall bought six long Uzbek knives at the tourist stands near Timur the Great's mausoleum, which reminded me of Disney's *Aladdin,* but dustier, with more complexity in the elaborate calligraphy and tile, and a bit faded. We picked our way through the prayer mats and people kneeling and praying to look at the fountains, the tilework, the snaking narrow corridors and passageways that took one's breath away with the sheer beauty and lushness of pattern and color. I was ashamed that I found myself thinking that *Aladdin* was more vibrant and exciting. Perhaps it is true — if people are exposed to the shiny, fake commercial image first, are they disappointed when they see the real thing? Will people who have been to The Bellagio in Las Vegas be disappointed by the real thing in Italy? I didn't know if we should act as though we were praying too, just out of respect. Thankfully, the souvenir shops allowed us an opportunity to avoid that dilemma. I bought scarves, hats, pashmina scarves, many things. Now I wish I had bought more. Marshall bought knives and more knives.

When we went back to the little Samarqand airport to fly back to Tashkent on the 1960s vintage Tupelov two-engine plane with little curtains in the windows, Marshall asked me to put his knives in my carry-on bag. I didn't think anything of it until the Uzbek airport security said, "You can't take these knives on board!"

"But they're just tourist knives," I said.

"It makes no difference! These are a security risk!" Of course he was right, but I didn't much want to admit it. Finally, a deal was worked out. The pilot agreed to carry the knives with him in the cockpit.

After the flight was over, he strode down the aisle with an armload of shiny, curved scimitars and very Persian-appearing knives.

" *Voshi nozhi, voshi nozhi* (Your knives, your knives)," he said, as the passengers identified their knives and placed them in their bags.

As we drove back to the apartment, I noticed a woman cutting open a watermelon with a long scimitar-type knife she might have bought in Samarqand. Later, on the same road, I saw a man selling large bags of unshelled peanuts. I couldn't help but think of my hometown in Oklahoma, just thirty miles from the annual Rush Springs Watermelon Festival, and five miles from Mason's Nuts, which featured bulk peanut shelling for all the peanut farmers in the area. November is deer season in Oklahoma, the time when every pickup truck features a gun in the gun rack, and a knife in the backpack. Lots of similarities, but the two places could not possibly be more different.

I didn't buy my beautiful red velvet coat, with its sequins, gold braiding and tassels, in Samarqand. I bought it at a market in Tashkent — the one where we sat in the *chai-hana* as the professor asked if he could sell me his books.

When we returned to the apartment, Marshall was up and pacing back and forth in his room.

"Open the door, Mom!" In a flash of horror, I realized that I had inadvertently locked him into his room. His bedroom used to be an extensive balcony, and the door was an outside door that automatically locked to the "outside" which was now the bedroom.

"Mom, I'm going to need a lot of therapy after this one!" he said as he bolted toward the bathroom. A few minutes later, he emerged. "You LOCKED me in the bedroom! I couldn't get out! What were you thinking? I am going to be psychologically scarred for life!"

He seemed fairly forgiving about it all, and not too wounded. At least his bladder didn't rupture. He did mention that he was at the point of peeing over the balcony, but there were people outside and he thought they might see him.

At that moment, Marina ran upstairs to tell me that we needed to go to the office immediately. She had managed to get an audience with USAID, and she wanted to present a "Protocol Agreement" to them. Later in the day, as we sat around a table in a tall, circular Soviet-era government tower, I began to have the familiar trapped feeling I always have when I am asked to do the impossible.

"Susan, with your contacts you can get us the funding for these projects, right?" the Uzbeks asked me. The USAID representative looked at me. I explained I was on vacation and I didn't really have any idea about specifics, but in a general sense, I wanted to support cooperative activities. International trade was just my backup plan. I was more interested in the gold deposits and in the privatization of some of the oil and gas operations. That was simply from a theoretical point of view, though — I am such a small player that I could never expect to actually be involved in any large-scale efforts.

Knives, hats, robes, women's roles, towers, lost messages, isolation, oil, gold, motherhood, life.

What does this have in common? Loss, for one. Interesting how neither one of us ever found the least practical use for our expensive educations. Does it matter? What is practical, anyway? I think that the fact that you are willing to listen to me right now makes the investment worthwhile.

Love,
Susan

December 21
Norman, Oklahoma

Hi Tek,

You'll never guess what happened. Westhorpe offered me the job! I am so excited! Wow. This is great. I love the place, the people, the job description, and I get to dress up in a military uniform. True enough, uniform is optional, but I like the idea of wearing it. Maybe I'll get to participate in some body fluid rituals. (joke). Well, if so, that would be a welcome change of pace. (!)

Now the big question is, how will I get up there? I'm so eager to make the big move, to look for a house to live in. I just can't wait. Westhorpe Falls, population 5,000, is very cute, and there are beautiful and picturesque houses with basements, attics, and two or three stories. And, it's only 12 miles from Montpelier. You were right. Even though the population is only 12,000, it has a lot of shopping and good libraries, thanks to the universities and the fact that it's the state capital.

Marshall told me he's very excited, too. He loves Vermont in the summer, and he wants to get into skiing and snowboarding.

I went over to Mom and Dad's house to tell them the big news, and they were unpacking a box that our cousin William had sent. It had Christmas presents in it — a handmade wreath made of fresh spruce branches and wild berries, some deer meat, a slab of moose meat, and wild raspberry jams. It is just too sad that William never had a successful relationship. His marriage only lasted a few years, and he doesn't travel enough to meet anyone. The fact that he is an accountant is a good thing, and he also has his small business in making maple syrup and selling it to non-Vermonters.

Now, to be honest, I think life with William would be impossible, but that's just my opinion. He is too parsimonious — he's the epitome of the "miser" Vermonter who hates to spend any money at all. But, he's a good guy, and there has to be some female out there who would be just right for him.

Before I make the move, I'll have to buy some warm clothes and some boots that won't slip on the ice and snow. You've always talked about how much you want to live in Vermont — perhaps you can go with me!

I have your Christmas present for you whenever you're ready. Do you know if we have to go to Todd's house again for this holiday? Thanksgiving was horrible. I don't think I could stand another dinner like that — Todd's "humor" when he announced to everyone that I must have mad cow disease, and that's why I'm so eccentric. I'll never forget when he told a guy I had invited to dinner with the family that I was disgusting and that I used to starve myself to be thin, but was a failure because I was always fat and ugly in high school, and that all his friends always considered me a "total dog."

I should try to go out of town or something for Christmas.

Talk to you soon,
Susan

December 25
Norman, Oklahoma

Dear Tek,

Merry Christmas! I would tell you in person, but with the ice storm and the roads completely impassable, I can't. The phone's gone dead, too. So, I'll write you this little Christmas note.

It's horribly icy outside. When I woke up this morning, and I could no longer hear the distant hum of trucks and traffic on the highway, I knew that the "dangerous winter storm" that had been predicted by local and regional weather forecasters was no joke. I don't often think much of the fact that my house is within a kilometer of a heavily-traveled interstate highway until the sudden lack of traffic makes me aware of the fact that my thoughts and my inner voices are starting to increase in intensity to take care of the void. I suppose it is similar to living, centuries ago, near a major river such as the Mississippi. You get used to the sound of the water flowing, and if it were to suddenly stop, you'd drive yourself mad with your own thoughts.

I've tried calling Gordo, the pumper on Wanette, to see if we've had any production problems. I'm glad we are far enough from town to be able to have diesel-powered pumps. Electric pumps are quiet, but in this case, we would have serious problems, especially if lines began to freeze.

It's quiet. I am unprepared for silence. I am also unprepared for lack of mobility. The streets and highways are covered with an inch of ice, and it's impossible to drive on them. They will be that way until we get some warm weather. That's Oklahoma for you! No one has the least idea how to handle ice and snow. Offices are shut down, stores close early, and people shiver in the dark as the weight of ice causes tree limbs to fall on power lines, thus cutting off electricity. Happy Holidays, right?

At least we have electricity, phone lines, and heat. But this silence! I can just hear you now — "Well, Susan, you had better get used to it. You're moving to Vermont in the dead of winter. They get snow and ice too, you know!"

But winter weather in Vermont is not like this. It doesn't make you feel absolutely cut off. Or, maybe it does — perhaps it is even worse, with short days, darkness at 3:30 in the afternoon in the winter, and the knowledge that your nearest neighbor is miles away down a dark and slippery road.

I remember the summers we spent at camp. It always seemed a bit strange to call a two-story, three-bedroom country house — with loft bedroom, basement, full bathroom with running water and septic tank, situated on 500 acres of land — a "camp," but that is what everyone calls their summer "place" in Vermont. I'll never forget what an accomplishment it was for Dad to buy the land, and I think that he thought that having the family there for part of the year would instill in us the values that made his family self-sufficient, hardworking, independent, with values that privilege education, professional endeavors, economic prudence, family support, creativity, entrepreneurship, and intellectual freedom.

But, really — who actually owned the land? Of course, the English immigrants weren't the first inhabitants.

Needless to say, the settlers were taking land from the indigenous inhabitants, the Mohawks and Seneca Indians, who were not pleased at all. Further, French trappers had made a habit of taking the resources and selling them. The French-Indian War had been fought near there, and the region was still hotly disputed. Which European expansionist government would get it? The French? The English? The Spanish had never wanted that area (unlike Oklahoma), and the Dutch were further south.

Later waves of newcomers would not consider themselves to be allied with an empire headed by a king or a queen who would applaud their individual effort to expand their realm. Future arrivals to the "New Land" or to "America" would be independent agents looking out for themselves, filled with utopian dreams of inventing new identities for themselves and (at times) their families. I have to say that it was much more customary for individual immigrants to abandon families back in Europe (or wherever) and to start over. If you think about it, that is a terrible legacy for us here in the US. It's worse than Australia! Instead of being descended from thieves, murderers, and uneducated criminal classes, our nation is descended from people capable of (and willing to) kiss good-bye their wives, children, aging parents, brothers, sisters, etc. No one likes to talk about that, though.

Here, the roads are silent. Marshall is at his dad's house. The electricity has been flickering on and off. The dog is cold.

Well, Merry Christmas! I'll bring your presents to you soon!

Love,
Susan

ON PEOPLE USING PUBLIC PLACES TO DISÇUSS PRIVATE THINGS

January 5
Tulsa, Oklahoma

D:

I'm sitting at Giga Bytes Internet Cafe and Bagel Shop killing time before I have to go make a presentation to try to convince employees at the Tulsa Worldcom office that they should sign up for a degree in "Administrative Leadership." I'm not looking forward to it. There is a lot of tension there. The employees are disgruntled and suspicious of management, due in large part to hiring and firing practices. Worldcom is a typical multinational telecommunications company that runs nice glossy ads of smiling people and spews warm, fuzzy talk about how "we love people like all of us!" In the meantime, they refer to their employees not by name, but by cubicle number. They tape all their phone calls and monitor and log all their computer activity. But, hey, it's a job. For awhile, at least.

What invariably happens is that, as an outside person called in by management, I get dumped on by frustrated employees. The first thing they do is accuse my company of not fulfilling its obligations. Since my company has no obligations to them, and we haven't said anything or done anything (yet), I never know what to say. It is really, really unpleasant.

To add physical misery to emotional misery, it's icy outside. I'm afraid I'll have to make the drive home in a sleet storm, which is not a pleasant thought, considering that people go 85 miles per hour on the highway, regardless of conditions: rain or shine, light or dark, dry, wet, or icy. I'm not feeling sufficiently suicidal to be looking forward to that!

There are three computers hooked up to the Internet cable modem service from "Charger Cable." Good. These are very fast Internet connections. Hmmm. I may try to download some of the news videos I never get to see on my computer because my cable-modem service is always clunky and slow. What I really like are the celebrity scandal websites.

Now I'm reading a little card taped up to the monitor: ABSOLUTELY, POSITIVELY NO PORNOGRAPHIC OR HATE-RELATED SITES ARE TO BE VIEWED IN THE CAFE AT ANY TIME.

Well. Good for them! I wonder what qualifies as a hate-related site? Neo-Nazi and white supremacist sites come to mind. I wonder if the "Jihad in Chechnya" site I looked at is considered hate-related? I was curious after I came back from the border of Dagestan, after having peered out across the Caucasus mountain range separating me from the ugly, twisted, horror-hole they call Chechnya. I personally think that Jihad-in-Chechnya.com is a very weird, fake site. I mean, who would actually put up "martyr stories" on the Internet? Who would actually put up stuff that suggests that to sacrifice oneself in the name of Allah is a good idea? I'm secretly hoping it's some sort of nicely-baited trap to catch jihad-crazed masterminds. How terrible, how horribly tragic. One time I was in Baku and my interpreter pointed out Chechens in an Internet cafe. I didn't know if it was true or not, or what it meant. Were they trying to earn a living and escape the refugee camps? If I owned an Internet cafe, I wouldn't want to be affiliated with that madness. I suppose that the Internet cafe could be liable for crimes committed or planned through their computers. I don't know.

Not much action in this Tulsa, Oklahoma Internet cafe. It's nothing like Baku — there, one got the impression that there were people with some sort of weird hidden agenda. (Unless it was just my overactive imagination.) Here, there's simply the sound of freezing rain hitting the pavement, a woman preparing a huge batch of bagels in the glass-screened kitchen, and a couple seated at one of the formica-topped tables. These are tables for two, each with a cut glass vase holding a half-dozen peach-colored silk daisies. There are ceiling fans, Victorian-style tulip-shaped lamps, and a little bar where you can go and refill your styrofoam coffee cup with all the coffee or machine-generated cappuccino you can possibly drink as you type furiously into cyberspace.

It's a calm place, moderately cozy, with a radio on a country-western music station playing in the kitchen. It's "pink noise" to cover the clicking of keyboards (only my clicking — I'm the only one actually on a computer), and a tense conversation between a balding guy and his fake-blonde wife. I say "wife" because they are talking about their kids.

"You know, your voice can be just as abusive as mine," the guy is saying. "You just won't admit it because you're not loud. Your abuse is different."

I can't hear her response. I'm trying to imagine what she does when she has an "abusive voice." I think of a vicious family argument — he's yelling at her for taking night classes at the university instead of staying at home to be a "good mother" or for having changed her mind about going on vacation with him, or any of the million or so ways to avoid the real problem, which is that they don't like each other very much any more.

"You know. Your voice gets sharp and you are cutting with your words," he said.

She's responding again. I'm straining to hear what they're saying, but I can't hear anything at all. What does she do when she's mad at him? Does she hiss at him like an indignant cat? Does she get on her hind legs and whisper in harsh, sibilant, reptilian tones? I remember how I used to piss off my brother. I wouldn't yell at him when he made me mad — I would smile at him in a bland, unacknowledging way, and then I would say to him, "I'm sorry. You're just boring me to tears. Could you try to be a bit more dramatic? Perhaps you could howl in pain or threaten me. I would prefer you to threaten to hurt yourself, if I have a choice. I'm not in the mood to be hurt."

Of course, those were the mind games of a teenage girl. I wonder what mind games this grown woman has developed over the years? People can be pretty interesting after years of practice on a person whom they have grown to dislike, or worse, to consider a parasite or a barrier to their personhood (whatever that means — "barrier to personhood" is something I read in a self-help / self-esteem building book).

The bagel-maker has just cranked up the country western music. I can't hear anything at all. Too bad. Perhaps the bagel-making woman didn't want to hear the conversation. Perhaps she thought it would spoil the appetite of the people in the cafe.

A man has just struck up a conversation with me. He's a tall and moderately husky guy, sandy hair, little half-beard, muscled-up arms, a gold crucifix on a thin gold chain around his neck. He has just moved here from Maine, but his family is originally from Massachusetts. He has the accent of a Massachusetts guy of Italian origins, and he's cute. He says he's dying of boredom and it's really hard to get to know people. Hmm. Nice strong arms. He says he was working in a tannery until mad cow disease struck and the tannery shut down.

That's interesting. As far as I know, there's only one tannery in the US. He must have worked in it. At least that's what they used to tell me in South America. They said that was why there were so many shoe manufacturers in Argentina, Brazil, and Paraguay. In fact, I went near a tannery — it was putrid! Apparently, the chemicals they use are horrible. Wow. A tannery. I immediately thought of all the cute shoes I bought in Paraguay — handmade, copied directly from Italy. Maine is home to many famous shoe manufacturing concerns — Bass being one of the most famous. Apparently, much of the handstitching was done in individual homes as piecework.

The tannery closed down due to mad cow disease? Well, that's really sad — I guess that means a lot of women won't be able to make money for their kids, etc.. God knows there are few enough jobs in Maine, Vermont and New Hampshire, particularly in the winter months. In fact, I remember my uncle's girlfriend used to do handstitching of shoes. She lived in New Hampshire. Her daughter wanted to study photography and Russian.

The husband and wife are leaving. She didn't look angry when they first came in. She looks pretty pissed now, though. I can only imagine the cutting, nasty remarks she'll say to him. She'll probably try to think of a different way to say them, or at least deliver them in a different manner, just to save face, just to give the impression that he was wrong.

The husky, hunky guy talks to me again. His name is Joe. He gives me his phone number. I wonder what it would be like to hang out with him.

I'm wearing a black sweater, black pants, and a gray jacket. I wonder what would have happened if I had on a t-shirt saying I HAVE SEX ON THE FIRST DATE, or, I LOOK BETTER NAKED. I'm not kidding you — there are actually t-shirts that say that! In fact, *Marie Claire*, a women's magazine, paid two women to wear them to a bar and to come back and report on the response they elicited. They both reported the same thing: lots of attention, but the guys who responded were creepy. They rated the guys — they ranged between 0 and 2 on a scale of 1-10. But at least they had pulses. That's better than what I've got — not to say that I am having sex with dead guys, but to say that MEMORIES DO NOT HAVE PULSES.

Okay. Time to sign off & to wish you a WONDERFUL NEW YEAR!

All best,
S

January 10
Norman, Oklahoma

Hi Tek,

It's just too predictable. Too, too predictable. It was so predictable it was sad.

Do you remember how I told you how much I hate driving up to Tulsa? I've been trying to market an interest in a coalbed methane deal on our Okfuskee County property. In the meantime, I've been talking to a friend who is developing a training program for the "Worldcom Leadership Project." Worldcom has 5,000 employees at that location in north Tulsa, and the atmosphere is horrible. You can feel the anger beneath the surface, the frustration of enraged employees who are tired of being told that they have "at will" contracts, meaning that the company can let them go ("right-size" them) at any time, with no notice. Over the last year Worldcom has laid off more than 1,000 employees in Tulsa alone. They expect to lay off 1,000 more in the upcoming year. It's crazy.

Anyway, you ask — what's predictable?

Human nature, that's what. Not the good in people, but the bad.

If you know how to entrap people with their own greed, you'll go far. Today, my friend had her contract stolen out from under her by a competing training company. The competing training consultant is feeling good right now. He won't once the Worldcom powder key blows up on him and disgruntled employees use him as their surrogate to punish their double-dealing management.

Nothing motivates someone more than the idea that they can get something for nothing.

Now, if only I could figure a way to apply this to my life. Let me think. I am very sick of the fact that the city sanitation service only picks up trash once per week. Hmm. Here's an idea. I think I'll pull out my old Gateway computer boxes, put trash and garbage in them, then tape them up as though there were a computer inside. Then I'll set it outside on the curb in front of Lil's house next door. Lil died six months ago at the age of 92. Imagine — a 92-year-old living alone! She had a heart attack and died at home. Sad, but at least she wasn't stuck in one of those horrible nursing homes for the abandoned elderly. Anyway, she's dead, so she won't care. I'll put the box outside. I'll bet someone steals it! Heh-heh. They'll get what they deserve!

I can't even improve myself. God knows I've tried.

Well, time for bed. Let me know if you can get together for lunch sometime this week.

Love,
Susan

January 13
Tulsa, Oklahoma

Dear Tek:

I should have known better. It was too good to be true. I had met him during my trips to Tulsa, and after several weeks of having lunch together, he asked me if I wanted to have dinner sometime. I like to call him Buck. That's not his real name, though.

Buck picked me up at my hotel — even brought flowers — we watched CNN a bit, talked about work, then headed out.

"Where do you want to go?" he asked. I suggested Los Alamos — a restaurant I used to enjoy when I was meeting with our working interest partners on the oil and gas prospects in Cleveland County.

After we walked in, I noticed that the place had declined a bit since then. The neon coyotes and the turquoise and coral jewel-toned leather chairs were gone. The frosted glass saguaro-motif windows had been replaced by "Coors On Tap Today!" and, to my horror, I discovered it was one of the few restaurants that actually allowed smoking. Once seated in the stinging blue haze, the waitresses were, if not downright surly, at least indifferent.

"You know, you only live once," Buck said.

I was watching a couple of guys in cowboy hats challenging each other to eat jalapeno peppers and chase them with mugs of beer.

"And there are some things in life that one deserves — it's the very minimum."

The man in the white straw cowboy hat was smirking at his friend. The jalapeno in his hand was at least four inches long.

I looked at Buck. I had no idea what concept or idea he was trying to express. He had never seemed particularly philosophical while we talked about training courses in conflict resolution.

"Sex every day. That is one thing —"

"What? I couldn't hear you." It was very loud, and they were playing some sort of "classic" I vaguely recognized. "Free Bird" or some other 70s cliché. I took another sip of my cheap but good Chilean wine.

"SEX. At least once every day," he said. That time I heard him. So did people at the next table. Smoke stung my eyes. Wine. Chips and salsa refilled.

"That's what you think you deserve? Like some sort of inalienable right?" I asked.

"Don't you think that everyone deserves to be happy? How can you argue?" he said. He was very serious.

The guy in the white cowboy hat was getting ready to chomp down on his jalapeno. His friend, a shorter guy in a brown cowboy hat looked at him, momentarily expressionless.

"I'm a man. I'm not getting younger — I need it. And, let me tell you — I like older women. My first time was with an older woman. She was Russian," my swimming buddy said. His jaw was clenched, and he stared intently at the votive candle in front of us. Silhouettes of worn horses and cowhorns were etched into the table. It was suddenly very obvious to me what the deal was.

"Are you married?"

"I will not lie to you. Yes, I am."

"How many children? Where's your wife?" I asked. It turned out he had two small children, a wife and a mother-in-law at home. According to him, his wife and he were "like roommates." I wondered if he knew what a tired cliché that was.

"So. You think I can somehow help you? Have you thought about preying upon your student interns?"

"Oh, no. That would be wrong," said Buck.

"Don't you have a right to them? After all, you are stronger than they are, aren't you?"

He had no idea I was outraged. Apparently, he was incapable of detecting sarcasm in a female voice.

I couldn't believe he would actually think I would be interested.

"What would your wife say?" I asked.

"Oh, she wouldn't mind," he said.

The guy in the white cowboy hat turned a bright shade of red, gasped, and groped for his mug. Tears streamed down his face. His friend burst into laughter.

I looked at Buck. He wasn't an unattractive man, and I had been very encouraged by our brief conversations. I had high hopes. I never expected this.

I put my hand on his knee. "What would you do if I told you I had no pantyhose and no panties on. What if I said we could sneak into the ladies' room, lock the door and no one would know..."

I could feel his knee tremble.

"Yeah. Yeah. I could do it. It wouldn't take long. Thirty seconds. And then I could be ready again in 15 minutes," he said. I had a mental image of a male rabbit caught in the act.

"That's supposed to be appealing to me?"

I finished my wine. My mind wandered as he talked about his inherent and indisputable rights as the male of the species. Before we paid the bill (or, more accurately, I paid the bill, since all Buck had on him was two dollars cash and an expired Diner's Club card), I grabbed his knee again and looked deeply in his eyes.

"Too bad we can't. There's a line to the ladies' room," I said.

On the way back to the Doubletree where I was staying, it occurred to me that such heavy-handed teasing may not have been such a great idea. He suggested we stop by his office for a minute or two.

"No. I need to go to the hotel and I need to think about things."

"What do you have to think about?" he asked.

I contemplated jumping out at the stop sign where he would have to stop after we exited the interstate. There was a telephone and I would call the hotel and they would send a cab for me. I could maintain my dignity, perhaps. It probably wouldn't be necessary, but it was an option.

Fortunately, he took me to the hotel without incident. The halo I had attached to Tulsa and its male population was completely undeserved, I decided. Further, I could see that my need to compete with men and "beat" them (being a smart ass) wasn't healthy sport.

The next morning, I bought a jar of jalapenos. Then threw them away. I couldn't stand watching them swimming around, turgid in their own juice.

Love,
Susan

January 14
Norman, Oklahoma

Re: on why I can't accept the job

Dear Berthold,

Just when I was thinking everything was okay and I had resolved the dilemma of the big move from Oklahoma to the northwoods of Vermont, and I had convinced myself that my 16-year-old son, Marshall, would be better off without me here to complicate his life, I had a conversation with him today at lunch that made me see things in a different light.

Actually, I don't think this comes as a surprise. I can just hear it — "What were you thinking, Susan?" — when I told you about Marshall and the fact that he said he didn't want to move with me, and the fact he said he'd come to Vermont in the summers.

In fact, Marshall told me at least a dozen times that I should take the job. He insisted. He even told me he'd never forgive me if I didn't take the job in Vermont. He'd be okay here in Norman, he said.

That's what he's been telling me. And that's what I've been telling myself. Plus, I tell myself that there's not much I can do, anyway. Sixteen-year-old guys aren't little boys any more. They're young adults. His dad has promised him a car. That's his contribution. I pay for orthodontics, contact lenses, dentistry, dermatology, clothes, shoes, incidentals, computers & skateboarding stuff. Before that, it was paintball. Before that, rollerblading gear.

When his dad and I split up in 1989, Marshall was five. We decided that joint custody would be the best thing. Actually, it wasn't really what I wanted, but his dad said he'd take me to court, ruin me financially, and tell the whole world that I was a crazy, fucked-up whore, and he had evidence to prove it, if we didn't do it his way. To tell the truth, I was afraid of him. I had a fairly interesting job as international operations analyst at Kerr-McGee Chemical Corporation in the pigment division, and I had just earned my master's degree from The University of Oklahoma. It was a nightmare. I just wanted the nightmare to be over. So, I agreed to joint custody, which meant we split custody — we traded weekends, and days of the week. So, the supposedly amicable arrangement quickly turned into a painful, gut-wrenching back-and-forth — on the surface, it was okay, but underneath, it meant a rotten, festering, emotional scabbiness that never, ever healed. I felt abandoned, abandoning, LOST, at least three times per week. Every time I took Marshall to his dad's house, and every time I sat in my empty house and folded his clothes, cleaned up his room, I felt a terrible sinking feeling.

My sister had a friend in a similar situation. She dumped her husband and he started getting skinny and weird. He started obsessing over a married Filipina who grew up in migrant worker shacks all over the Southwest — a description which makes her sound heroic and I suppose she is, except I think that she's being played by her own self-marginalizing routines, which make her vulnerable to the advances of a flabby white boy redneck, who, on paper, is a mainstream professional). She got a divorce. He moved in and gained about 50 pounds on her Tagalog cooking. In the meantime, he was a bully to the son the mother could not protect. My sister's friend could do nothing.

My sister's friend's ex beat his kid so hard he had bruises. She said she took photos and tried to use that to "encourage" the dad to behave. Of course it was extortion, *chantage.*

But, it's confusing. About a year and a half ago, Marshall announced to me that he wanted to stay with me "only on weekends." He wanted to live at his father's house during the week because his father "provided structure" and "forced him to do his homework." Plus, Marshall claimed that I could never get him to school on time, and consequently, he was failing his first-hour class. "Won't you give me another chance?" was all I could think to say. He wouldn't. His resolve was adamantine.

That precipitated a downhill slide. I started to feel very sad, rejected, overwhelmed, exploited. He would come over to my house on weekends — that was true. But, he was always accompanied by friends, most of whom spent the night. I rarely had one-on-one conversations with my son. The situation was further complicated by the fact that I often taught weekend classes, or was out of town. Our "quality time" could be measured in nanoseconds.

At times, when he'd sneak out through his window to skateboard or to hang out with his friends, I'd blow up. My brain would shrink to the size of a pea, and I'd start thinking in only the most primitive of terms — "If you don't like me, then I don't like you! Just go live with your father!" Sadly enough, I'd even say that — hoping to elicit some sort of response. I did. He responded by spending more time with his friends.

When I first contacted Westhorpe, Marshall had just said he'd like to move with me if I got a job. My sister said she was eager to move to Vermont, and in fact, was actively job-hunting. It seemed to be a move made in paradise. I thought it would be a really wonderful way to start over. I relished the idea of not having this absurd weekends-only (but with friends!) schedule. He'd be at my house. No more back-and-forth stuff with the ex. But, when it came down to the wire, Marshall said he "wished me only the very best" and "Good

Luck in Vermont!" and then he added that he would not, under any circumstances, move.

My first reaction was to feel terribly rejected. "Why don't you want to go with me? Don't you love me? Have I failed so abjectly?" I didn't actually ask the questions. I knew that the answer was that I had, in fact, failed in a fairly spectacular fashion, in the only task that had any meaning to me. I'm a piss-poor mom — that's what a good self-respecting American mom would say, I fear. I buy Marshall what he likes to eat with no regard to nutritional balance (okay — I do buy multivitamins), and I'm all too ready to buy him a digital nanny — Nintendo, VCR, TV, a computer with cable modem access, software, digital camera, etc.. He'd be better off without me, I told myself. Plus, he'd be safe with his dad. His dad could deal with discipline and all that. Teenagers need a *mano dura* as they say in South America. *Mano dura* is "strong hand." Never mind that I've always thought of it as "strong-arm" and not necessarily positive. Oh well.

Later, after endless discussions with my parents, my sister, my father (especially my father, who is absolutely worn out by all this, but who, paradoxically, seems to like the fact that I'm seeking his advice), I arrived at the conclusion that Marshall will be fine here in Norman. He has family and friends, and sufficient financial resources to do well. I, on the other hand, am not doing so well. I've used my job as a substitute for family, and, as a result, I've advanced, but I'm not likely to be able to advance further, given the structure of the organization where I work. I have been traveling too much to maintain close friendships, and the people I consider my best friends tend to disappear as other attractions come along. My romantic life has been very annoying and unsatisfying. I am, in fact, one of the disconnected ones in society. My best friends are my parents and my sister. They are, in reality, my only friends. Other than that, the phone is silent, with the exception of calls from one worthless, erstwhile boyfriend who hangs onto me because I have gotten him easy, high-paying jobs. It's self-interest. In the meantime, he cheats on me. Who am I kidding?

Vermont was looking better and better. It looked like the answer to many, many prayers. I could start over. Marshall could move with me. We could be a cool, tight little family unit. At least that was the fantasy.

But, today at lunch I realized it's very serious, and I can't really afford to leave Marshall. To be honest, I realize that, he's all that means anything to me at all. My wonderful "career" is something I do to keep from starving, and to be self-sufficient. That is something new. My first year to be financially independent and completely self-supporting occurred in 1996 at age 38. Pretty amazing. Before that, I was dependent upon my dad. I worked for him, and he paid me.

As I ordered coffee and an omelette with cheese, peppers, and sausage, he selected quiche lorraine and cheesecake. We sat down and I asked him about the "semiformal" dance last night.

He said it was fun — they danced, etc.. I asked what kind of music they played: Was it techno? Top 40? Euro-dance? He said he didn't really remember, but that the last song was about suicide.

I have to say his answer surprised me — I asked, were there teachers there? Did they react? He said he didn't know.

Then I asked him if anyone had committed suicide at his school so far this year? He said, "No, but there have been a lot of attempts."

"What kind? How?" I asked. I wasn't too surprised, but I felt very sad about it all. Being a teenager is rough, and it's especially hard in Norman. Norman is a very status-obsessed place — status quo and pecking order. I found my years at Norman High to be excruciating. I always felt I was different from the rest of the students. Okay, I realize that sounds as though I suffered from a very intense narcissistic personality disorder. The truth was, I felt different, but in a negative way. Not special, not chosen. Marked. Twisted. Stained. Suicidal thoughts are never far from a person who feels unworthy of existence.

"Mainly pills," he said.

"Do you ever think about suicide?" I asked my son.

He took a bit of quiche and averted his gaze. I swallowed. He swallowed. My stomach knotted up.

"Yeah. A lot," he said.

"Have you ever tried?" I asked.

"Yeah, but not seriously. Just enough to scare myself," he said.

I felt my lips trembling as my eyes filled with tears. I sat silently for a moment.

"How many? When?" I asked.

"Well, when my dad really pisses me off. Like when he yells at me and tells me I'm a greedy bastard. And then I think that nobody cares. One time I took eight aspirins. Once I took a bunch of Tylenols. After they took out my wisdom teeth, I took all of the painkillers at once."

A thousand questions surged into my mind. Has Marshall seriously tried? Are there many like this? Are you desensitizing yourself? Are you practicing? What next? Do you find life so painful?

I didn't know what to say. I drank some coffee and stared at my plate.

"I guess it's pretty normal to think about suicide sometimes. Especially if you feel completely powerless to change your situation," I said.

"Yeah," he said.

We talked a bit longer and my stomach finally unknotted itself. How can I possibly leave? Maybe some miracle will occur and he'll start getting along with his dad. I doubt it. His dad is what my friend Michelle refers to as a "health-ruiner." Eventually everyone around him starts developing severe physical problems that have some sort of psychosomatic origin. I used to think that applied only to the wife. Now I realize he's equally toxic for his child.

Hey, but I have some part to play, too. Obviously I've failed to make things better for Marshall. Maybe that can change. It won't if I'm in Vermont, though.

It's a great job. It's a great place. The people are top-flight. The challenges and opportunities are fantastic. Vermont itself is beautiful, idyllic.

It is also very far away. It is easier to fly to London from Oklahoma City than to Burlington.

And, what good will I be in Vermont if I'm worried out of my skull about Marshall. What will he do if I'm gone and he only has his friends for support? Right now, I'm some sort of a pressure-release. He said that when he thinks about suicide he believes that no one cares. How can I help him build up enough self-esteem and self-confidence to realize that someone DOES care?

The next day, in the car, Marshall talked to me. "Life is easier for simple people," said Marshall as we drove to his dad's so he could pick up his skateboard tools and loosen up the too-tight trucks. "Simple people just take life as it comes, and they don't think about it very much. Every day, every minute is the same for them."

"That's interesting," I said. "And isn't it ironic — sometimes what someone considers their deepest flaw is really the key to their most valuable talent. They have to have one to have the other. And suddenly life isn't simple."

"Yeah. Like my friend Kelsey. She's really creative. She's also really up and down a lot, emotionally. She changes, and she's not simple at all. She sees life differently. But if she saw life the same as everyone else, she wouldn't be so talented. So she's stuck. She's not simple."

"That's amazing. You see it very clearly," I said. I was feeling sadder and sadder.

We drove down the tree-lined streets, shaded by the interlacing branches of elm, oak, and sweet gum that darkened the street with their incredibly complex patterns. Two-week-old piles of dirty snow and ice were slowly melting under the thin January sun. I dropped Marshall off at Jackson Elementary School. I noticed his friend, Chad, was waiting for him, skateboard under his arm. "I'll call you later, Mom. I've got the cell phone."

As I drove off, I realized I needed to stay here in Norman, if for nothing else, to be available for phone calls from my only son, Marshall.

Sincerely,
Susan

January 20
Norman, Oklahoma

Dear Tek,

Just as I was unloading the dog food, trash bags, milk, Pop Tarts breakfast pastries, and Little Debbie's miniature cakes from the Honda, a red car with darkened windows pulled up. I thought it was my ex Nathaniel's car, but it was around 10:30 p.m. and too dark to tell. Nathaniel rolled down the window and said "hello."

I was a definite "deer in the headlights." I didn't react for a second, then responded with the basic, "Hi, how're you doing." Marshall got out of the car with Chad — "Chad's spending the night." I said, okay — then announced I had just returned from the store with food.

The typical weekend torture-fest was more or less over, or at least smoothed out for the night.

All the weekends are the same. I wonder where Marshall is. I suspect I know where he is. I think of him skateboarding in places posted "no skateboarding" and guys yelling at him, like at Hastings — "Can't read the sign?" with the rejoinder, "You mean the one that says NO SKATEBOARDING?" And then I think of his friends who skateboard — the drug use, the dysfunctional family lives, the semi-suicidal urges, and my complete helplessness.

Marshall just walked in and said, "Mom, I read your e-mail you sent to me. You try to make me feel guilty."

What do I hate about this so much? Why do I feel so frustrated? I think it boils down to helplessness. When I was traveling more, it was easier. There were nice distractions — exotic locales, foreign languages, danger (!), and of course the necessity of performing the job(s) at hand.

You said I should absolutely and completely avoid traveling right now. Well, that's a nice thought, but my business is all about the contracts I have with the IMF, World Bank, and national agencies. I like the work — yes, there's travel, but there are also long stretches at home, where I have a completely flexible schedule and can be available to Marshall when he needs me. At least that's the idea. I'm in town — writing reports, proposals, training materials. Actually, it would be great if Marshall and I could have lunch every day, or at least a cappuccino. We can sit back, ponder life, and talk about philosophical things.

For some reason, he's never in the mood to do that!

Instead, I get a weekly weekend torture-fest. I'm feeling desperate. I wish I had friends — someone to talk to besides dear old Dad & Tek. It's good to be close to one's father and sister, but I see myself doing a self-infantilization routine as I crave security and escape.

It's all so difficult and sad. I think I'll go off and have a good cry. About what, I don't even know. I just feel sad, alone, desperate, unwanted, ugly, fat. And there you have it.

Love,
Susan

January 22
Norman, OK

Hey Tek,

I talked to Gordo. It looks like we're going to have to replace the storage tanks on the Wanette field. That's going to be an $18,000 expense. We're producing 16 barrels of oil per day from that lease. Eventually, we'll be able to pay for the tanks. But, I'm just hoping that remediation and reclamation expenses aren't too high. I didn't see any evidence of spillage, but we'll have to pay for soil samples and submit them.

There's no future in this. It's not like it was in the "good old days." The little person just can't make it in the Oklahoma oil field these days. You have to branch out — go international.

I'm going to Bolivia in a few days. They are (in theory) seeking outside investment. If I can find a good opportunity, assemble a group of investors and get involved in a project there, perhaps my dream can stay alive. Who knows.

Do you want to go with me?

Love,
Susan

ON THE STREETS OF LA PAZ

La Paz, Bolivia
January 23

D:

The *cholita* woman who sells lottery tickets and changes money outside the hotel has offered to come home with me and to be my live-in cook and maid for $26 per month. We had entered into a conversation because she had sold me some very nice fossils — trilobites — that can be obtained near here.

What a bargain — $26 per month. Of course, it's legally problematic. It's also ethically problematic.

"What would you do with your kids?" I asked. I looked at her face. She had the beautiful complexion of the Bolivians I met, with smooth skin and pink cheeks. Wearing the typical felt fedora atop long dark braids, and clad in a bright pink sweater over multiple skirts, fluffed out as though she had crinoline skirts underneath; she was postcard perfect. She had told me earlier that she had five children. I had met her oldest daughter, who helped sell lottery tickets and fossils after school.

I was feeling a bit exhausted. My visit to Yacimientos Petroliferos Bolivianos, the Bolivian oil company, was inconclusive. No one seemed to find any information on the joint ventures they had described to me in a letter. It was frustrating because I have potential partners, and it could be something that could save the business.

In the meantime, I'm doing the microbusiness, economic development / trade thing, in order to have two possibilities, not just one.

Her offer was morally vexed, but it was soooo tempting. Imagine. I would be coming home every day to a freshly swept house, with shiny mopped floors, polished furniture, and the smell of disinfectant and Glade air freshener. It would be heaven. As it is now, my house smells of stale potpourri and whatever new designer soap I have put in the bathrooms. The dog would be nicely scrubbed every day, my collection of tiny perfume bottles neatly arranged in the glass cases I bought for them, and the back porch swept clean of pine needles. Lovely!

"I don't want to *desanimarte* but I think that the paperwork required would make it pretty impossible," I told her. In her traditional dress, she wouldn't blend in too well in Oklahoma. However, I'm sure she would be absolutely adaptable. She would not be like the characters in V. S. Naipaul's short stories. It was a shame that I would not be able to help her.

People need to have chances to realize their dreams.

Of course, sometimes people are saved from themselves. Thank God I've never received everything I've wished for!

It is an incredibly gorgeous day. The air is clear, with a sky like a robin's egg, so intense and pure that I feel I'm inside a painting from the Italian Renaissance. I guess it's always like that at 12,500 feet. I don't know. The people on the streets off the Prado near downtown La Paz are crowded together, going wherever they are going, selling whatever they have to sell. One person has a handful of ballpoint pens, one has a little case of handmade earrings, another has bottled water. Other items for sale include pocket calculators, cosmetics, Brazilian candy, glasses of *refresco* dipped from a bucket. I wish I could lose myself on the street, among all the people. From my perspective, these are people who do not hassle anyone. They simply struggle to survive in the only manner they know how.

Of course, in economic development terms, this is classic underemployment. Peddling trinkets on the street is definite "go nowhere" work.

Selfishly, I'm happy for the "go nowhere" work. It means that I can buy cool handcrafted silver earrings for $2 apiece, a hand-loomed wool sweater with bright pink and green llamas standing against a backdrop of an acid yellow Illimani

Mountain, the tall Andes peak featured in many travel brochures.

Never mind that the day-glo bright dyes are not colorfast, and have tinted my neck a scary green, and have permanently stained my t-shirt. Poetic justice? Probably.

I have a number of places to visit here in La Paz. Most appointments were made two days ago, as I did informal market research at the Expo-Cruz in Santa Cruz. I'm here to help develop a marketing plan to help local microenterprises supply local large enterprises, and to find ways to export new lines of products. The bottom line is that it is "demand-driven" production.

Too bad that most people still tend to have the "Field of Dreams" idea — "Build it and they will come" (!).

Usually, they don't.

I'm breathing in the thin air, well-fortified by two steaming hot cups of *mate de coca.* That's a hot tea made from coca leaves. It's a weak stimulant, and supposedly helps one deal with the altitude.

I think I'll explore the narrow, cobbled streets where doorways open directly onto the street, and where you can see the dark interior you will have to pass through before you emerge into courtyard rooms filled with light and plants, where an *empleada* quietly sweeps the floors or slices vegetables to cook for dinner.

Yesterday I visited one of these little museums, and I saw maps and exhibits which illustrated the two disastrous wars that Bolivia had recently been engaged in. The first was one with Chile, when Bolivia lost its coastline and mineral resources in the region called the Littoral. The second war took place in the 1930s, when Bolivia fought Paraguay for a region called the Chaco. Bolivia lost both territory and men in the two wars.

No wonder the Bolivians feel they are long-suffering — fate's victims. With conquista, wars, colonization, *latifundio* (a kind of sharecropping system), and more wars, the Bolivian people really have suffered. Of course, some groups suffer more than others. The indigenous Quechua, Guarani, and Aymara populations paid a big price. Now it's time to give them a way out. Microenterprises could be the way. At least I hope so !

My knees feel a bit rubbery from the altitude. I'll write more soon. Tomorrow I go to Oruro, which is a silver and tin-mining town. It's at an even higher elevation than La Paz. I'll need lots of *mate de coca*!

Love,
S

ON WHY FORMER POLITICAL PRISONERS MAKE GOOD DRINKING BUDDIES

Oruro, Bolivia
January 25

D:

I'm staying at the Hotel Terminal here in Oruro. It's thirty bucks a night. That's pricey for this part of the world. They have running hot water and heat. That's good. I need to get the green dye from the sweater I bought on the streets of La Paz off my neck eventually — I'm running out of turtlenecks and high-collared blouses.

I hope to be able to go into a tin mine. I have heard that it's strictly forbidden for women to go into the mines. We'll see.

Hotel Terminal. Who names these places? All I can think of is "Hotel California" (you can check in but never, never leave). Terminal. End of the line.

Actually, they call it that because it's near the bus station (the terminal).

Fernando and I took the "jumbo" luxury bus from La Paz. It wasn't what I was expecting at all. I was thinking pigs, goats, perhaps a chicken or two would be messing it up in the back. Instead, there were uniformed attendants and an "in-transit" movie. How am I going to be able to tell anyone that I sat and watched *The Sixth Sense* dubbed in Spanish while riding in a bus in the Bolivian Altiplano? No one will believe me!

I dropped off my bags in my room. Fernando lives in Oruro, so he checked in with his family. Then he said he'd show me the town. We went to a little café and ate dinner. Then we went to a small club where we sat in a dark booth, drinking a sweet, port wine-like liquor that was made from grapes grown in the south of Bolivia. The music was mellow and sad, with many American pop love songs, which I translated into Spanish for Fernando. I found out how Bolivians drink together, and the little rituals involved. They say *chin-chin* at the beginning, then drink together; that is, they only take a drink when the other takes a sip. Each time, they pause to wish each other *salud.*

It occurred to me that such a rhythm of drinking was set by a mutual acknowledgment of the need for the next *trago* — the next pain-assuaging sip of alcohol, to mitigate the realization that we travel through life in such a solitary manner.

Drinking that way creates a nice harmony. It's definitely a communion of sorts. I felt very comfortable.

Fernando waxed poetic at one song, and told me it reminded him of his days in prison as a political prisoner.

Well, needless to say, that got my attention.

"Wow. Really? Were you tortured? What was it like?" I asked. I was hoping that he would excuse my perverse curiosity as some sort of weird Americanism.

"Yes. I was tortured. But not much," he said.

"How can you say 'not much'? Isn't all torture the same?" I asked.

"No," he paused. He picked up his glass of port wine. *Salud,* he said. I picked up my glass, joined in with a breathless *salud* and took a sip.

"I'm alive," he said. "Many were not so lucky. They died. Either by torture, or because they sewed up their mouths and refused to eat or drink."

I was absolutely horrified. I hadn't realized that Bolivia had experienced repression. This sounded eerily similar to other countries. Bolivia's neighbors, Argentina and Chile, immediately came mind.

"I was released because I was not important. I was helping with organizing the laborers, and trying to form a *sindicato* (union), but they didn't care. Plus, my uncle was influential in the government, and they did not dare go too far."

We were seated in the chilly club, near the glowing coals of charcoal in a portable hibachi the waiter put near us. It was comfortable, and I imagined how miserable the nights must have been in prison.

An hour slipped by before I knew it. The conversation was fascinating — we discussed politics, prison conditions, philosophy, history, and torture techniques.

"I really must return to my family now," said Fernando.

On the walk back to the Hotel Terminal, I noticed that the stars were as bright and twinkling as Christmas tree lights. They seemed absurdly close. The air was dry and thin.

That night I slept well, but with weird dreams of being on a bus driving through the Altiplano, listening to a group of musicians play the *lambada* and sing of torture.

When I woke up, I was ravenously hungry.

And now it's time to meet Fernando for breakfast. Maybe he'll show me his scars.

Talk to you soon,
S

January 26
Oruro, Bolivia

D:

Hello from high-altitude Oruro — at 16,000 feet, if you don't feel euphoria, you've got a headache!

I'm here to visit the tin-mining and smelting operations. I'm also intending to buy products from *micro-empresas* — microbusinesses — that specialize in artisan goods, handcrafts, textiles, etc. that take advantage of indigenous crafts. They're unique, and have been passed down from generation to generation.

Production of the items is not a problem. Finding markets is the challenge. Everyone seems to have the same "Field of Dreams" mentality, no matter where they live. "Build it and they will come!" Sure! Dream is right. Without adequate outlets for the goods, there is no hope for long-term success. Money down a rathole. But, we're trying to help the women and children here. It's tough in a mining town where the mines are dangerous and depleted, and the price of tin is in the dumps.

Speaking of marketing — it's the same old story everywhere. The guys who develop the market outlets will be the ones who flourish. Who do those people tend to be? The people with marketing ability are almost exclusively from the privileged class, and they are the ones with access to capital and education.

No surprises here — the rich get richer, and the poor are exploited.

I'm amazed at how creative people have to be to get ahead. Fernando explained to me that he's an artisan out of default. He's a mining engineer who couldn't get a job, so he started to make items of pewter (high tin content). Here in Oruro, things tend to be simple — one could even say absolutely utilitarian. You go inside a door, you sit at a dusty table, and you look at people around you, most of whom seem to wear a coating of dust on them. They are quiet, reserved people. At least that is what they appear to be around me. Fernando says that when they drink, though, they drink to oblivion. The violence, pain, and passion come forth. It can be frightening to see, not because it is expressed in violence, but because you see the self-destruction seething inside.

Time to chew on a coca leaf, huh?

This is the place where they used to pay miners a part of their salaries in coca leaves. The miners would chew them as they worked in the mines. It took away their hunger and their cold. Everything on the surface was a monotone of tan dust and gray rocks. Underneath, in the bowels of the earth, in the *socavones de angustia* (mine shafts of misery), it was dark and scary. Offerings to the earth gods were everywhere in the mines, or so they said. As the miners went to their particular operations, they would make an offering to the little *cacique* (the chief).

I asked Fernando if I could go underground. He looked shocked. "No. You'll bring bad luck. You'll make the *caciques* angry." He looked nervous.

"But I have a degree in geology. I'm here to help find investors," I said.

"That is even worse. You'll bring outsiders in," he said. "The gold, silver, and tin belong to the *caciques.* The miners have made a special deal with them — and, if they keep them happy with enough coca, the *caciques* won't be angry. That's what they believe. I believe it, too."

"Okay." I examined my chapped hands. I pretended to not have said anything.

Fernando led me into the workshop he wanted me to see. They made *diablito* masks, he explained. I nodded, eager to see what it was. I understood the Spanish word for "little devil" but I had no idea what he might be referring to.

To my surprise, the *diablito* masks looked like the dragon masks used at the Chinese New Year. But this was Bolivia, I reminded myself. I wondered about the influence and sharing of cultures. The masks were used just before Lent, during the Carnival parade. They were used in a dramatic reenactment of an old Quechua or Aymara Indian myth, "rehabilitated" after *conquista* with Christian characters. The drama symbolized the Biblical story of Lucifer and the bad angels fighting with the good angels, before God cast Lucifer and his beautiful, but bad, angels out of the heavens. Once Lucifer hit the inferno, he turned into a devil, and his cohorts were other devils.

The Diablito Dance is the ultimate dialectic: good vs. bad with a synthesis at the end, which could take the form of sleeping off a hangover (!).

Molded of *pâpier maché* and a substance created from crushed bones, they were painted with glorious, day-glo colors, decorated with mirrors, sequins, and other festive baubles. The masks were created in all sizes — in miniature for decorating around the home or place of work, or full-sized to be worn by a person. Electrifying combinations of geometric designs and patterns, and the fuschia, cobalt blue, chartreuse, hot pink teeth, snakes, eyes, mouths burst from the masks. Each artisan expressed his or her vision of the universe and the meaning of Carnival, and as a result, each mask was absolutely unique.

I'm from the so-called First World. However, I never wanted to get involved in the exploitation game. Nor did I want to simply visit the touristy places and view prepackaged experiences from a tour bus packed with Americans. I wanted to immerse myself in Bolivia, understand the people, the geology, the cities.

I suppose that I can never transcend my own identity and heritage. I may think that I can, but I cannot do anything about the way that people will react to me. They refuse to let me out of the little box they have put me in.

As a result, there are often hidden agendas in every conversation. It's enough to turn one paranoid.

I'll write more soon — much love,
Susan

January 26
Oruro, Bolivia

Hey Tek,

I think you made the right decision in not coming with me to Bolivia. I'm looking for opportunities for joint ventures, but people are evasive when it comes to details. Sure, they'll take my money. But, they won't give detailed information, or let me see properties or have up-to-date mining reports.

I'll bring back some inventory for the gift store, but that's about it. I feel overwhelmed. I'm going it alone. I'm learning a lot about the culture and the history of this place. It's instructive in that regard. However, I have an overwhelming feeling about the impossibility of it all.

Sometimes I think I'll just go home and try working as a cashier at Wal-Mart or something. At least it would be stable and predictable for Marshall. Of course, I wouldn't be able to pay bills, so that option is out.

That's when I start thinking of doing the French Foreign Legion thing and moving to some place at the end of the earth to give English lessons. Could I survive? No. Probably not.

I think the altitude is getting to me.

Love,
Susan

January 31
Norman, Oklahoma

D:

It's SuperBowl Sunday. I'm not watching. Are you? Somehow I doubt it. Actually, that's what I like about you. You are utterly indifferent to professional football, except to comment about how it relates to American culture.

I'm sorry I haven't e-mailed you in a few weeks. To tell the truth, I've been nervous. I'm afraid you'll criticize me for losing my nerve and not taking the job in Vermont. I hope you don't mind that I send you e-mails. I need to talk to you, or at least communicate the best way I can.

I even dialed your number before I realized what I was doing. I guess I love futility.

Last Sunday, I came home to a locked downstairs bathroom and the voices of Marshall and Chad inside. I was a bit embarrassed. I turned on the stereo and starting playing Radiohead's *Kid A* as loud as possible without the neighbors complaining. Then I tried to make more noise —then the phone rang. It was for Marshall.

"Is Nash home?" asked the female voice.

"Marshall, you've got a phone call," I said. "And, by the way, what are you doing?"

"Having sex with Chad," said Marshall.

Chad shouted, "Shut up! No, we're not!"

Marshall emerged, hair coated with Cherry Bomb hair dye, Chad was Iguana Green. Just then, the doorbell rang. It was Chad's mother. To my surprise, she didn't seem particularly upset. She laughed.

"Oh you silly Chad! What will they say at school?" she asked.

"I'm so sorry — I had no idea they were going to do this — I never would have condoned it!" I said. "Plus, they got green dye on my freshly painted walls."

Chad's mom didn't hear the last part. She was busy hugging her son. I was envious. They seemed to have a healthy mother-son relationship.

"Mrs. Nash is giving away all her books, and I thought you might like some, Mom," said Chad.

"Uh, yeah, I'm moving to Vermont," I said. Chad picked up the two boxes of books on bioethics, human rights, and human dignity, all in Spanish, published by the medical university in Bogata, Colombia, I had visited a year ago. The medical school had a distance learning program for outlying regions, and these books were part of the required reading. The publisher of the texts was also the director of distance learning, so he had a captive market. At least, he used to have one. One of the professors was kidnapped, and the program was put temporarily on hold. And they had wanted me to teach in the program. Fat chance!

However, the idea of teaching bioethics in the Colombia hinterland appealed to me right now. I remembered when I traveled there a year ago, my parents had told me they would not pay a ransom, so I needed to keep that in mind as I discussed my itinerary.

Tek asked me how my decision-making process was going. She took the opportunity to tell me the same thing she always does.

"I think you should take the job. If you don't you will always regret it because you are a coward. You will never forgive yourself. This could be the only opportunity you'll ever have. If you don't get out now, you never will. You will grow old and die in Oklahoma, surrounded by cowboys, pickup trucks, child abuse, divorce, and ignorance."

Tek continued. "I've lost three pounds since January 1. I've been doing 200 sit-ups every day." She paused and looked at me. "What kind of exercise are you doing?"

"Nothing," I said. She looked appalled. "It's been too bad outside to run. Uh, I do the Stairmaster while I watch the *C.I.A. Files* on the Discovery channel."

Dad has suggested that I go on walks with him. He's 74 years old. I'm 42. Clearly there's a message in that.

"Just make that call tomorrow. Call them up and tell them you accept. Marshall will never forgive you if you don't go," said Tek.

"But I won't see Marshall for months at a time! What if something happens?" I protested.

Dad's feedback was: "You've raised him for 16 years. That's all you can ask for. There's nothing you can do. Plus, you and he clash. He will appreciate you more in the future if you leave now."

"But I just received two major commendations from the World Bank."

"And how much did you get for your 'Innovative Development Program award?"asked my sister.

"A plaque," I said.

"Wow. Big deal. Maybe you can treat the office staff to donuts. Remember, you have no place to go but down. You'll never rise any higher here," said Tek.

I tried to imagine myself in Vermont without Marshall. Although all we did was argue, I would probably miss him. I thought of things I could do to keep from missing him. I could organize a creative writing group. I could get involved in volunteer organizations. I could revise the semi-pornographic novel I wrote in 1991 and showed no one. I could publish it under a false name and make money. I could finish my embroidery projects. I could take up ice-skating. I could travel on weekends. I could look up the Armenian guy I fell in love with in 1990 in Montreal. I could sign up for intensive Russian courses. I could sign up for remedial French. I could try to commit suicide by lap-swimming. I could try to commit suicide by cross-country running. I could take up skiing. That would definitely be the death of me.

Tonight, after Marshall came in from skateboarding, he showed me the bruises on his knee he got from trying to do technical skateboard moves on the wet pavement. It was raining, and had rained at least four inches in one day.

"Doesn't it hurt?" I asked.

"Yeah. It will hurt more later, though," he said.

I fixed a pizza. I spread out salami on top, thinking that maybe it would taste like pepperoni. Yesterday, at the corner grocery store, salami was on sale for $1.50. Pepperoni was around $4.

Unfortunately, the substitution was a failure, and the salami tasted thick and lunch-meaty.

"Do you think Sammy would like some?" I asked. Sammy is our "cinnamon" beagle — cinnamon because his spots are a cinnamony blonde color. You remember him — he howled at you when you came over to visit me after I passed my general exams for the Ph.D.. You were still studying for your exams. You were in the living room and he saw you through the sliding-glass doors and started his ridiculous baying / howling bark.

"Mom, do you think that your cooking is what's giving Sammy seizures?" he responded.

I paused. "Yeah, it's possible." I put the pizza in the refrigerator. I wouldn't feed it to Sammy. I would probably eat it after my round on the Stairmaster.

On my way back to the kitchen, I heard the "plop, plop" of water falling from the ceiling. Sure enough, all the repairs I had done a couple of months ago were in vain. The ceiling was leaking again. The new roof was not keeping out the rain. The new ceiling was sagging again. The water was making a stain. And there I was, crying again.

I hope everything's okay in Elko.

I'll try to call in the next few days.

All best,
Susan

February 5
Norman, Oklahoma

Dear Aygun,

It was a nice surprise to receive your e-mail! I was very flattered that you happened across the website I did for my "Love and Madness in Film and Literature" course, and even more excited that you'd like to ask questions for an article you're writing for a magazine in Istanbul. I realize that it's in Turkish, but I'd still love to see a copy. I have a number of Turkish friends, including a friend who's in Istanbul now to teach in a local university. He is a professor at a university in New York and has done a great deal to promote contemporary Turkish literature in the US.

Anyway — to answer your question — most people have known of someone who was either erotomanic in some way, or have at least known someone who was victimized by the often absurd, often comic, and sometimes darkly terrifying and dangerous delusional disorder.

Technically, erotomania is a variant of delusional disorder, which is described by the *Merck Manual of Diagnosis and Therapy* as "the presence of one or more false beliefs that persist for at least one month. Delusions tend to be nonbizarre and involve situations that could occur, such as being followed, poisoned, infected, loved at a distance, or deceived by one's spouse or lover. Suffering from a delusional disorder can be problematic for the individual, and lead to negative consequences. The *Merck Manual* describes behaviors and beliefs ascribed to erotomania: "In the erotomanic subtype, the patient believes that another person is in love with him. Efforts to contact the object of the delusion through telephone calls, letters, surveillance, or stalking are common. Persons with this subtype may have conflicts with the law related to this behavior."

In most cases, the disorder manifests itself as quirky and sometimes socially embarrassing beliefs that can result in uncomfortable responses from friends and loved ones. Thank God I've not suffered from erotomania — at least as far as I'm aware.

However, I've seen it around me. I'll never forget the 50ish poetry professor with thinning hair and a budding paunch who was convinced that all his female students were in love with him. The truth was, nothing could have been further from reality — most of his students loathed him — his pompous pronouncements that there were "no great women poets in the 20th century" and "just because a woman committed suicide did not make her intrinsically interesting." He also had an annoying way of drawling his words when he spoke so that his comments, no matter how innocuous or benign, became instantly patronizing. I began to wonder if eroto-mania is almost an acquired syndrome in academia, at least among aging professors. I think it manifests itself within the aging female professor population as a delusion (fantasy) that younger male professors are sexually harassing them.

For some perverse reason, I liked the guy — perhaps because he made me see the ordinary through completely new eyes, and a fresh frame of reference. While taking an independent study course in poetry writing with him, he suggested that we take a road trip through the rural regions of central Oklahoma, and the downscale fringe suburbs that flanked Oklahoma City. We passed trailer homes, trash heaps, rusty cars, weather-beaten billboards advertising beer and whiskey, car lots, rundown roadside diners, and mile upon mile of trash-lined rural roads.

"Just look at the industrial decay and clutter," he said. "It's gorgeous — it's like an earthwork or a living abstract expressionist painting — a *tableaux vivant!* There's nothing like it — the muted grays, browns, and fading neons!"

When I began to look at Oklahoma's rural poverty as the contents of a painting or an art project, I was able to distance myself from the immediacy of it all. Somehow the poverty in my own backyard that frightened me lost its sting. It became exotic. Perhaps that is the charm of the delusional disorder.

Likewise, all the 20-something young women who worked hard at being desirable and desired, could have been deeply threatening to this professor, who would never rate high on anyone's desirability index — not for looks, or for personality (!). How much easier it would be to convince oneself that they all were secretly in love (with an emphasis on the "secretly"), but for a myriad of reasons could not actually permit themselves to display or even express their true feelings.

It reminded me of Nabokov's Humbert Humbert, whose horror of fully mature women triggered his perception that their daughters (specifically Lolita) were in love with him, and shamelessly trying to seduce him. Of course, the question is, in *Lolita*, whether Humbert Humbert is truly an erotomanic pedophile, or simply a man with an advanced case of delusional disorder (erotomania) that has crossed the line into an active form of schizophrenia, replete with auditory and visual hallucinations.

As the *Merck* manual points out, erotomanic behavior can be frightening. Stalking is often perceived as a logical response to rejection. Sadly, the person being stalked never even met the stalker, and thus could have no idea whatsoever that someone was watching them and judging their behavior to be rejecting, indifferent, disrespectful, or even cruel. It is usually a shock to the object of the delusion that such feelings exist. When they find out, they soon realize there is little or nothing they can do to alter the erotomanic person's delusions and thought processes. Film examples are many and include *Fatal Attraction, The Crush, American Beauty, Sweetie, Taxi Driver*, to name a few. Many times, the erotomanic delusion goes hand in hand with the desire to "save" or "rescue" the person from a situation (or clutches of a loved one) that is "keeping them apart."

I personally think that this sort of delusion could be almost incurable. What can you do? Mild erotomania could be harmless and make the world a more enjoyable place. What are we without dreams, anyway? But full-blown delusional disorder of the erotomanic variety? All I can say is, look out for a long and difficult road ahead. Or simply RUN (unless, of course, you are the one suffering from the delusional disorder).

If you have any questions, or would like clarification, please don't hesitate to contact me.

Sincerely,
Susan

February 5
Tampa, Florida

D:

Here I am in Tampa, relaxing on the back deck of my hotel room which overlooks one of the three golf courses on this property. It's a real scam. In order to attend the conference one has to stay here. Needless to say, it's absurdly expensive. I suppose it's okay if you play golf or need a suite for entertaining potential clients. But, if you're traveling alone and just want to get some business done between meetings, it's ridiculous. The only consolation is that there are alligators lurking in the rough (consisting of moss-draped cypress trees and swamps) & occasionally they go after a golfer. Bring your clubs. Don't bring your dog.

I'm in a huge suite which I got after complaining about the first room I had because it reeked of dead cigar smoke which was making me nauseous.

I think that giving me this room was an act of retribution.

Imagine — a full kitchen, a dining area with a huge table with eight chairs, a huge living room with two sofas, three occasional chairs, coffee table, five end tables, five lamps. That connects to a sitting room with another sofa, a huge television, coffee table, two armchairs, two end tables. The bathroom and bedroom are another story: two tiny twin beds, and a bathroom that has no bathtub, just a shower made from a vinyl kit that is so small you can barely turn around. Thank God I'm not overweight (okay, not much). It doesn't even have shower doors. Instead, there is a curtain which, when I arrived, reeked of mildew.

So, I called and complained (again). Then I had to call and complain because the "hospitality armoire" which is stocked with tiny flasks of liquor "for your comfort and convenience" had been pilfered. The bottles of whiskey were open. One had only about an inch of alcohol left in it. I looked at the price list and discovered that it was $18. I didn't want to be charged for it, so I called and complained (again). Then later, the toilet didn't flush correctly, so I had to complain about that.

On the second day here, they gave me a gift certificate for $25 for food and beverage. I presume it was an attempt to shut me up.

So, now I'm propped up here, killing time until the exhibition hall opens (with a reception) and watching people play golf. What a boring game. I'm hoping for an alligator.

Today's newspaper was filled with news of all the new layoffs and fears of a recession. I guess that's really why I'm here. I have a sense that if I push myself as hard as possible to have the skills companies need, I'll be able to find a job. Now that so much emphasis is placed on Internet skills, it seems like a good idea to keep up with it all.

I also had the idea of putting up a website that describes the fields we're producing and the wells we have planned in Oklahoma. Perhaps we can attract investors. Plus, I think I'll put up a listing of my trips, and opportunities I've found for investment. Maybe someone would like to partner with me, or hire me to check out the leads.

But, at the same time, I realize I'm just going through the motions. I completely agree with you — there's no way to beat the system. It eventually consumes one, and trying to be or stay "middle class" is more or less a thankless and ultimately futile task. In order to "be" middle class you have to "look" middle class, and have all the requisite toys and equipment. That means a car payment, a cable modem access bill, a new laptop every 18 months, new software, the "right" kind of wardrobe, the "right" kind of luggage, the "right" kind of accent. It also means living in the "right" neighborhood and having your children do the "right" activities. The only way to do that is to have a lot of credit card and other kinds of debt, which of course, makes one play right into the hands of the system.

It makes the small little trailer parks here in central Florida look pretty good. They're tucked in little palmetto groves with raked gravel lawns and potted bird-of -paradise flowers all around.

A slender Asian (Cambodian?) maintenance guy just left the room. He came in response to my latest complaint — the toilet was not flushing correctly. It takes about three flushes to get a piece of toilet paper down it. I don't think he agreed with my diagnosis. He went in and emerged after about two minutes: "Toilet running good, ma'am."

I played along and pretended I believed he had fixed it. "Thank you!" I sang out to him in my most cheerful and innocuous voice.

I'm sure he did nothing and that it will still require three flushes for a little wad of toilet paper.

Yeah, so back to the trailer parks. I regret having made snide remarks about the cool little trailer park next to the apartment complex where you were living. At least it's single-family living, and it's quiet. I was afraid I'd lose grip on "middle class" life. Now I don't care.

That's part of what appealed to me about Vermont — I imagined living like my cousins do. My cousin William lives in the house his great-grandfather built in the 1880s. It has eight bedrooms and a wood-fired furnace in the basement. My dad says it's a firetrap. But, he can live on about $6,000 per year, which is about what he earns between his CPA business and selling Vermont maple syrup.

When I interviewed in Vermont at Westhorpe, I drove up to see William. He wasn't there — he was out hunting. I noticed that the house next to him was up for sale. My mom told me one could probably buy it for about $20,000 — less than what my Uncle Eddie and Aunt Cora's house went for. They died, too — my Uncle Eddie died in a nursing home after a series of strokes. My Aunt Cora died about three months later in the flu epidemic that went around about a year ago. Their house — three floors, five bedrooms, a cellar, side barn, big gravel driveway — sold for around $30,000. The same house in Norman, Oklahoma would be around $200,000. Who knows what it would bring in Elko?

I have to say that it was very sad to drive up there — it seemed very dark and lonely. Night was falling and the area seemed utterly desolate.

But, if someone had around $50,000 saved up, they could get a loan for the house and pay around $350 a month, then live on the interest. It would be a fairly isolated life, but there would be a certain amount of peace about it. And, one wouldn't have to live in the game of always wondering when your company would be bought out and you'd show up at work just to be ushered to your office by two uniformed security guards, watched by them as you packed your personal belongings (instructed not to touch any files or the computer), and then escorted to the door after giving them your keys, cards, and anything else. This happens everywhere, and it doesn't even matter who one is. One can win "Employee of the Year" one day and then the next, be laid off.

I remember hearing a piece on work and future trends on National Public Radio around 12 years ago. The guy was right on target. He said that in the future the worker would be like a mercenary soldier — he'd be hired to do a job, and he'd bring everything needed to do the job with him. He'd have his own gun, his own bullets, and he would have obtained the training and skill level he needed on his own. He'd do the job — no benefits, no retirement, no medical insurance — then he'd collect his pay and move on. The mercenary could be a woman, too (BTW).

And that's the way we all are. Have Laptop, Will Travel.

Wish you were here — maybe we could walk around the golf course at night & dare the 'gators to come & get us.

!!!

All best,
S

February 8
Tampa, Florida

D:

I'm still in Tampa — it's a nice day — warm and sunny. I'm sitting outside at the Pepperoni Grill eating an informal "brunch" of ham & pineapple pizza, coffee, and Innisbrook Cookie ice cream. Three tennis outfit-garbed, tanned and quite attractive women are sitting at the table next to me. They appear to be in their late fifties, early sixties. I hope I look that good when I get to be their age. They're talking about movies. They have New England accents. Right now they're talking about how much times have changed since they were teenagers. The most slender one, wearing a classic white tennis skirt and tennis blouse, with a navy blue sweater draped over her shoulders, is telling the others that she can't believe how open our society is.

There's a "nature trail" across the asphalt road from here. It appears to be a raised wooden walkway through a bit of swampland. I asked the server here if there are alligators.

Her answer was satisfying: "Yes, they're a big problem. Sometimes people think it's fun to try to hit them with golf balls. They don't realize the alligators will chase them. They run much faster than people. Yeah, it's a big problem."

I don't have any golf balls, just a plastic Easter egg with a software vendor's name inscribed on it. I won't throw it at an alligator. I'll save it for the office.

I don't know if you feel this way these days — it's amazing how "flat" I feel.

I don't know if it's depression or not. Maybe it's some sort of aftermath of the Westhorpe thing. So — here I am in the middle of a huge golf resort, attending a conference filled with guys who are "successful" and who, in theory, have something in common with me, at least on paper. And yet I have no interest. I'm alone, and I have a huge hotel room. I could have a fling (although it might be a bit cramped squeezed into one of the twin beds in my room). I could go on the prowl to be wined and dined.

Prowling seems exhausting. Plus, I feel bloated. I'd have to shave my legs and armpits. Too much trouble. Why bother?

The other night as I was moving from the cigar-smoke room to this absurd "hospitality suite" room, I realized, to my amazement, that the bellman had been talking to me for more than twenty minutes — that was after I casually asked him how long the property had been managed by Westin, and if he thought they might be trying to sell it. He started telling me about how he had worked at the resort for twelve years, and it was a nightmare now that it was managed by a large, worldwide chain. He then launched into talking about his dad, his childhood in upstate New York (Saugerties), his Hungarian grandfather who had a restaurant in Manhattan, and his mom, who is staying with him in Florida as she gets chemotherapy for her colon cancer.

He was cute. He had a nice body (from hauling a lot of luggage, I suppose). The way he acted, I had a feeling he may have wanted to continue the conversation. I gave him a tip, thanked him, and did nothing.

I blew it.

Why was that? There was my great opportunity for some human contact — some warmth and possible sexual gratification. But it just seemed unfulfilling — buying condoms, shaving my legs, drinking wine, getting tipsy, getting naked — I probably wouldn't have the nerve, and would just piss him off by teasing him, then saying I couldn't do it. And — what would we have in common? What would we talk about? What would we do? How would we relate to each other?

It just seemed awkward and embarrassing. No thanks.

I just picked up a flyer for the Salvador Dali Museum about 40 miles up Highway 19 in St. Petersburg. Maybe I'll go.

Last July I was in St. Petersburg, Russia. Why not visit St. Petersburg, Florida? Salvador Dali is not my favorite — he reminds me of an early glam-rocker. He was all about hype and self-promotion. Dali was a lot like the rock stars of today in the sense that he stole the ideas of the originals. Elvis stole music from the Black South. Madonna steals the music from the Black homosexual community. And so it goes.

Hey, maybe the bellman would like to go with me to St. Petersburg. Okay. That's a joke. It would be too much trouble. Besides, what would we talk about?

I suppose there are advantages to this state. As you pointed out — erotomania and obsession are a lot of wasted effort. The thrill takes a lot of manufacturing and self-delusion. It's a lot of work. It's just much easier to let it all go — although it's a bit sad to give up the dream — the dream of love, acceptance, and raw sex.

The downside is this dead inside feeling.

Any suggestions?

All best,
S

February 14
Norman, Oklahoma

D:

Here it is, Valentine's Day, and I'm desperately groping for a workable definition of "love." I love my mom, I love my son, I love my family — those sound culturally acceptable, but the sort of familial love they denote does nothing at all to explain the exalted "love" found in literature.

When I say I love my son, it is an emotion that surges in the wake of irrational bonding; a feeling that manifests itself in actions, both automatic and by design, that demonstrate an active nurturing, protecting, guiding, giving, and forgiving force.

At least that's how it seems on a good day. Sometimes that same "love" manifests itself as nagging, scolding, browbeating, jumping to conclusions, blaming, and self-justifying.

Then I feel guilty. I wonder if I've scarred my son. Who knows. People can be fragile. But, hey — maybe he deserved it (joke). I am at a loss — I remember myself at age sixteen (my son's age), and I think that in some ways I was worse than he is. I had fantasies of spending one summer traveling through Mexico alone on a third-class bus — the type holding pigs & chickens — just to see "hidden Mexico." I thought it would be fun. My mom said it was okay for me to go if I could find someone who would go with me. Of course, no one was even the slightest bit interested in my proposal.

At this point in my life, somewhat saddened and definitely gun-shy regarding love, I find myself hesitating before I embrace the mad world of double meanings and dissembling appearances that is the breeding ground of love. I want to proceed with caution, and I do not want to be hurt or make a fool of myself.

And yet a few months ago, something very puzzling happened. Despite my calm demeanor, my self-control (my self-repression, perhaps) I found myself in a weird situation as I killed time in the dusty-floored, crumbling, Soviet-era departure lounge of Kazakhstan Airways, waiting for a flight that would take me from Atyrau, located on the north tip of the Caspian Sea, to Budapest.

On the other side of the waiting area, I noticed that there was a crew of construction workers — probably Hungarian — sitting together. They were drinking vodka (it was eight in the morning) and laughing. I was imagining that they were eager to get out of Atyrau, which is a rather bleak place of wind, saline grit, industrial pollution, and crumbling infrastructure. I was sure they were ready to get back to a place that didn't have water rationing (water three hrs/day) and latrine-type toilets. I noticed a guy seated with them, and I felt my heart skip a beat and my stomach turn to butterflies.

There was nothing particularly remarkable about the guy — I did like his sense of style, though — overalls, t-shirt, interesting shoes, dark blonde hair pulled back in a ponytail. Of course, we had absolutely nothing in common — I was sitting there in a black blazer, black & white striped shirt, black skirt — Little Madame American, wearing her business travel gear to minimize hassles. He was either Russian or Hungarian. He looked Hungarian.

My heart was pounding. It was all I could do to keep from trembling. I couldn't even look at him. What was it? I have no idea. Was it mutual? I'm sure it was not. (I'm only saying that so it won't look like I have some sort of form of delusional disorder — some kind of erotomania — like the stalker who believes the stalkee is in love with him!) I didn't sit near him in the plane. Later, I didn't see him in customs. I still think about him.

Now that I'm back home, I regret my common sense. I wish I had run up to him and pledged to him my undying love, and begged him to marry me and come with me to the US. I hate it that I did nothing. I wanted to tell him — in extended and wordy refrains — all about how much I loved him — all in English, which would have been rather useless.

I didn't. I couldn't even look at him. But now I wish I had said something. The chance was lost forever. He was so gentle-looking and mild-demeanored. He had the sweetest, most forgiving & comprehending face I've ever seen. He was honest and good and kind (or at least he seemed that way). And I blew it. Why? I'll never know.

On the other hand, my family might have been a bit dismayed if I had dragged home a non-English speaking husband. That's assuming he accepted my bizarre proposal.

But still — was that the last time I'll ever feel that emotion? Maybe. I'm not sure why I even felt it at all. Perhaps it would bear looking into. Maybe it happened because I wasn't glued to the Internet like I usually am at home. While I was in Kazakhstan I had no access at all to the Internet. Maybe it was because I had just spent six days actually living life and interacting with people — perhaps the life I lead here is dehumanizing and has turned me into an unfeeling automaton.

What is love in the 21st century, in the age of the Internet?

Perhaps that's what I should really be asking, instead of pining for a man I only glimpsed in the airport of Atyrau, Kazakhstan, plunging myself into my own absurd reenactment of Dante's *Vita Nuova* — written as a tribute and love-testimony to Beatrice — a female he saw only once, having glimpsed her in passing on a street in Italy.

If only I had that morning in Kazakhstan to live over....

Your unstable friend,
S

February 25
Norman, Oklahoma

D:

I'm sorry I haven't been much of a correspondent lately. How are things in Elko?

Although I was avoiding meeting people, I did run into a guy in Tampa. We met at the poolside luau / barbecue hosted by the conference. He was fairly interesting to talk to. He's slender and tall, about 55.

He invited me to dinner. I didn't go. Instead of having dinner, I went to a bookstore to look for a novel written by an ex-CIA bureau chief. I think I am only attracted to louts and thugs.

Last night, I was watching American Movie Classics and *Bullitt* was on. I didn't realize what it was at first. It's really a great 70s film. Actually, was it even a 70s film? Maybe it was 1968. Steve McQueen was incredible. I remember him in *Sand Pebbles,* which had a huge impact on me.

I liked the existential chase scenes. It struck me that there is very little dialogue, and lots of sound effects — running feet, screeching brakes, huge engines. In that respect, it reminds me of *The Third Man.* But, of course, it has nothing in common with *The Third Man.* I loved looking at the 70s scenery — it is amazing how much things have changed and not changed. I remember that in the mid-70s, two big technological inventions changed the way we did business and thought of the world. There was the affordable xerox machine and electric typewriters with built-in eraser tapes. Xerox machines and IBM Selectrics — amazing, isn't it? It really did make a huge difference, though. Other things leapt out from *Bullitt* — polite flight attendants dressed in feminine outfits, jowly men with five o'clock shadows and no regard for their "look," ugly public architecture, a large and secure-feeling middle class. Have the changes in our society been for the better? Who knows.

Last Sunday, Marshall and I went to Braum's and while we were there, he asked for an application form. A friend of his works there, and he thought it might be a good place to work. Today, the manager called Marshall, they had an interview, and he got the job. So, he went down to the thrift store to get the type of pants he needed for the job. (I thought that was pretty cool of him.) So, he reported for work at 4 p.m.. At 1 a.m., I was starting to get worried. He wasn't back yet. Then, around 1:15 he dragged himself in — "Nine hours, Mom! Nine freaking hours!" Apparently there are only two jobs at Braum's — the manager and everyone else. So, he did everything — made shakes, swept floors, cleaned off tables, and did mountains and mountains of dishes. It seems to pay pretty well, though, as those types of jobs go. I was surprised to find that he was getting $6.50 per hour. That's more than an adjunct English professor, once you factor in preparation and grading papers. Plus, he got a thirty-minute break, and he got to eat. So, knowing his appetite, I'm sure he piled away at least $15 (retail) of burgers, shakes, fries, etc.. Actually, he makes more than a graduate student I know who works at the bookstore — he makes $6 per hour.

Any thoughts on jobs, careers, etc.? I'm going to Azerbaijan again in March — this time to lead workshops on how to build websites, design flyers, use digital cameras and make digital videos. It will be interesting — it will be in Ganja, which is fairly remote. It's a long way from Baku. Apparently, there isn't much heat at night, and the electricity is sporadic at best, except where they have generators. I'm going to get some of those fleecy pants to wear at night (!).

I hope things are going well.

Any good movies lately?

S

TURKISH BEER

March 5
Norman, Oklahoma

D:

I'm on my way to Azerbaijan. This time I'll be in Ganja — it's near Nagorno-Karabakh, and I'll be working with refugees who have started small businesses. Ganja is also a key hub for the Baku-Ceyhan pipeline, which, once completed, will be the main export pipeline for oil from the Caspian.

I have to admit it. I'm nervous. I can't believe how unenthusiastic I feel. Maybe it's because I'm burned out. I don't know. Well, I'm making a list of what to do and what NOT to do while I'm in Azerbaijan.

1. Don't drink Turkish beer. I have to remember this. Absolutely NO Efe's beer. Under NO circumstances. I have had unfortunate experiences with it — it tastes smooth and innocuous going down, but then, the dizziness! The headaches! The hallucinations! The last time I drank it, I had decided to stay up all night in my little hotel room in Baku. It was easier to do that, since my flight left at 4 a.m. and the driver would pick me up at 2 a.m.. So, hey, what a good idea — kill time & relax. So, I opened up the little refrigerator in my room and pulled out an Efe's. I also ate some nice

peanuts (although stale). You can't imagine how miserable I was — not just on the seven hour flight to London, but also on the 11-hour flight to Dallas! Never again — a headache, fever, malaise. All from the Efe's.

2. Don't go to transvestite dance clubs in Baku. Okay. I have to be honest here. I really enjoyed it. We went down the dark, crumbling concrete steps to a little bar with a crowded dance floor. It smelled like cigarette smoke, perfume, sweat, and mold. Men as slender as snakes were moving their hips and arms in serpentine moves which evoked the image of harems, Persian silks, and (of course I would think of this!), decapitated heads mounted on stakes on the outskirts of a city just invaded by Mongols. Ah, how romantic. If my breasts weren't so big, I could pretend to be a guy dressed up as a woman. But, maybe having a huge chest is an advantage. They seem false. True, I'm blonde and have gray-blue eyes and impossibly pale skin. Details, details! I would love to pretend to be a man pretending to be a woman. Perhaps it wouldn't matter so much that I am an utter failure as a real woman.

3. Remember — say NO first, and then say YES. I have a bad habit. When someone asks me to do something, I first say "yes." Later, I check it out, and if it looks impossible, I say "no." I'm afraid to miss opportunities. But, when I say "yes," it is sometimes difficult to extricate myself and say "no." I found this out in "affairs of the heart." I got myself into some rather unsettling messes, including marriage. So. I need to practice saying NO and then, after a lot

of haggling and negotiations, I can relent and say "yes." I need to practice this. Perhaps I can sit with a mirror and rehearse a few scenarios:

"Would you like to have coffee this afternoon?"

"No."

"Would you like to have dinner tonight?"

"No."

"Here, let me give you a gift! It is a silk scarf. May I give it to you?"

"No."

"Can you get my son a scholarship?"

"No."

"Would you like a necklace?"

"No."

"Would you like to travel with me to Turkey?"

"No."

"Will you marry me?"

"Yes."

"What? Great!"

"I'm sorry, I made a mistake. I meant to say NO. It was just a bad habit rearing its ugly head again. I call that bad habit the 'yes-monster.'"

"I don't understand. If this is your feeble attempt to be humorous, you have failed."

"No."

"What?"

"No."

And so on. If I replay that scenario a hundred times, perhaps I'll get it right.

And, now — you're in Elko. I'm still in Norman. How do you like that? It's weird. But, there was a lot of time we missed. I don't want to be overly sentimental about it, because you're right — we spent a lot of that time snarling at each other. We were both English Department graduate students where nothing seems to change, but then, everything changes — it's really hard to understand it sometimes. We were pretty nasty to each other. I don't even remember the years you were dating the woman who then went on to date one of her professors.

I miss you! What great conversations we had.

In retrospect, I suppose it was a lonely, pathetic time. And yet, those five years I worked on the Ph.D. were the best of my life. Right now, although I'm hanging on as a geologist, I'm still affiliated with the university. I sometimes feel as though I'm involved in some sort of long, extended post-doctoral program. I'm in a state of suspended animation.

I often wonder if I've made the right choices. And then, I think — who cares? And, what's a "right choice" anyway. I am sooo burned out. All I want to do is to sit in bed, read trashy novels and eat frozen pizzas cooked in the oven, which I then share with Sammy, my blonde beagle. The dog gets fat. I get fat. But, it's sort of satisfying to look out into my tiny backyard and see my incredibly obese dog, who no longer looks like a dog at all, but some sort of weird, aberrant pig with longer than normal fur and doggish paws.

I just got Arturo Ripstein's latest movie in the mail. I ordered it from Amazon.com — the name of it is *Carmesi Profundo (Deep Crimson),* and it's the story of a gigolo faux-Spaniard who goes around seducing (then killing) women in a Lonely Heart's Club who correspond with him. He meets a fat nurse named Coral who specializes in treating the terminally ill. She is so sexually frustrated that she does unspeakable things with her patients — she forces them to fondle her breasts, etc.. By the way, Coral is really fat. She's not just plump. To make it worse, the director puts her in dresses that make her hips look like a cement mixer. Scary. But, she and her fake Spaniard gigolo hook up (actually, Coral stalks him until he relents) as a team. They pretend to be brother and sister. He seduces the women, she helps fleece them. The only irony is that they never get much out of their victims. The victims wind up dead, though — Coral is jealous, and what does a Death & Dying nurse do when aroused into a jealous rage? You guessed it. Rat poison!

The movie is brilliant — it is grotesque, intense, and often funny. It's not tragic-comic in the way of Mike Leigh; it's not a supposedly postmodern world of chaos and apocalypse (as in *Natural Born Killers).* I'd say this movie is horr-onic (horror-irony). Hmmm. At any rate, I recommend it. It's supposedly similar to the 1969 film, *The Honeymoon Killers,* featuring the inimitable Shirley Stoller (famous for her frau-of-Auschwitz role in Lena Wertmuller's *The Seven Beauties).*

Talk to you soon,
S

March 6
An airplane somewhere over Europe

D:

I remember (maybe incorrectly) that you once said that *Titus Andronicus* is the only Shakespeare play that has any real relevancy for today's world.

The other day, I rented it — the version with Anthony Hopkins as Titus — and I watched it in all its twisted glory. Wow. Now I have to say that I liked the costumes — especially Saturninus after he became Caesar. But — rapes, human sacrifice, cannibalism, cutting off the hands of the rape victim, decapitation, and a father killing his sons in some twisted sense of duty and honor? Then he cuts off his own hand to save the life of another son — which is a waste of a perfectly good hand. It was so ghastly (almost funny) to see Lavinia trying to turn the pages in a book of Ovid with her stumps (arms now without hands), trying to speak after her tongue was cut out.

Woof. The movie was almost unwatchable. Did you like it? I am really eager to know why you thought it was the play for our times. Of course, I realize that if one reads the newspaper — especially with atrocities occurring in rapes, thrill-kills, etc. — it's easy to see what you meant.

It had an apocalyptic edge to it, and a kind of nihilistic gleefulness — as if the future were taunting the Roman past —a "nah nah nah you think you're tough now, but your wretched empire is about to collapse" sort of historical gloating. I'm sure that if *Titus Andronicus* were set in Washington D.C., and it revolved around a collapsing American political system, there would be a large number of fans. Everyone likes to see the bully on the block go down. *Titus Andronicus* could also be set in Moscow in 1989. Now that would be interesting! Perhaps Tamora, Queen of the Goths, could be Tamorancha, Queen of the Chechens, and so on. Titus Andronicus would be Tetya Andronikov.

Marriage choices were fairly ill-advised in *Titus Andronicus.* That is so true to life. Why do people make bad choices? I've made two choices. One was bad, the other was spectacularly bad. You know about the second. I would like to run away from that one. I like to pretend it never happened, and that I've been married only one time. Well, if only THAT were true! Actually, I don't know who I'm kidding — it was a short, gruesome marriage — the kind people love to gossip about. I'm not sure why I'm thinking about it now — perhaps I'm trying to understand what went on and why I am so unenthusiastic about commitments. I always seem to find something wrong with the situation and/or configuration.

I don't know why I never found anything wrong with the second marriage before plunging into it. I guess I knew it would fail, but I didn't have any way to avoid it.

But, I learned a lot — the painful lessons were something I suppose I needed. Also, if I had been a bit more positive about myself, perhaps I would not have gotten married in the first place — especially to such a loser!

Okay. Here's what your mother always told you which turned out to be true after all:

1. When Dad says, "That guy's a LOSER!" don't just argue with Dad. Look at yourself in the mirror and accept that maybe, just maybe, he has a point.

Of course, this always backfired for me. I looked in the mirror and said, "My god, I'm such a LOSER, too. We deserve each other. We are losers in loserville together." It sounded romantic.

2. Emotional intensity (read "sexual obsession") isn't everything it's supposed to be. Sexual obsession is not the foundation of a good marriage. On the other hand, there has to be something to keep you wanting to come back for more.

(Actually, sexual obsession sounds pretty good right now. But, I guess building a relationship on sexual obsession isn't healthy.

What do you do with the guy after you wake up? How do you take him to parties? How do you invite him to Christmas dinner with the family? And do those little bourgeois niceties matter? It sounds a lot more appealing to reject polite society's norms and go for the adrenaline flow. Where is sexual obsession when you need it?)

3. Consider the possibility that a nice, solid, traditional guy could actually be a nice, tolerant, understanding guy. Just because he's boring doesn't mean he's bad. And, if he's one of those control-freak types — can't bad boys be controlling, too?

Hmm. This is arguing against the notion that any relationships can or should stay intact, especially if "nice guys" AND "bad boys" will eventually turn out to be controlling monsters.

4. Your life partner should have at least some basic resources. He should have at least some sense of human decency. A guy who stays in bed for three solid days because he is "depressed" needs serious psychological help. Sex is not psychological help. Sex is a part of the problem.

5. When you find yourself talking about how good it would be to get away from it all — move to Montana and start all over — just the two of you ('cause you've jettisoned the kids somewhere back along the highway) — start worrying! This

is not healthy! True, it sounds romantic. Doesn't everyone want to reinvent herself or himself? Doesn't everyone want to escape from the cares and worries of life and go on an extended vacation and/or cross-country drunk? Even if you don't have kids, this option is bad. Eventually you wake up, and you're stone broke, hungover, jobless, and you look pretty foolish when you show up to look for a job. (How do you explain you've been hitchhiking and doing nothing for a year and a half? How do you explain the bruises on your face?) Maybe all romance is self-destructive. I don't know. The "falling off a cliff" feeling one gets with bad-boy (or bad-girl) love can be intense.

I have no idea what happened to the second ex-husband. Thank GOD we never had any kids. I should have known that I didn't feel good about any of it — meeting him, getting married within five or six weeks. I didn't want to introduce him to anyone, and I hated the idea of having him accompany me anywhere. And, I didn't like going with him to his stupid events.

Do you ever find yourself attracted to a person who seems to have the same demons as you? I have to say that I have been — I suppose the notion is that if I can help them work through their demons, then I'll work through mine, too. Plus, there's the acceptance factor. I think I'm being accepted. It never turns out to be the case, but I fall for it.

In the end, I think I gained a lot from the nightmare second marriage. I was so determined to prove him wrong that I pushed myself very hard to get jobs and earn more money. Actually, I sort of got myself into a trap — I was so busy trying to work, instead of feel, that I got into a bad pattern of spreading myself too thin.

But, at least I extricated myself, and now I have options. Actually, I probably have too many options.

How are things in your love life? I'm still getting calls from the Charleston dude, the one I met at the poolside luau in Tampa. Needless to say it's another disaster. But, I'll save that for some other day.

All best,
Susan

March 8
Baku, Azerbaijan

D:

I'm taking a few moments to compose my thoughts. I'm at the Mecca Hotel. It's my sixth trip to Azerbaijan. I've stayed here several times, and each time I am perplexed anew by this place — its official name is the Mecca Hotel and Islamic Research Center.

Now. Doesn't that strike you as a strange combination? Why would something be a hotel and an Islamic Research Center?

I gave up trying to figure out that puzzle. I finally concluded that Rafik, the owner, is trying to make this place as multipurpose as possible. Well, who can blame him? This is not exactly an easy place to make a living! Out of eight million inhabitants, one million are refugees. Out of eight million inhabitants, maybe 10,000 have a life that is comparable to the one they had during Soviet times.

There is a lot of despair and frustration in this country.

But, I'm not thinking about that now. I'm just looking at the new renovations at the Mecca. They have new dining room furniture and wainscotting on the stairwell walls. It's an attractive shade of pink, which makes a nice contrast with the white marble stairs and adds to the cheery, light-filled atmosphere. The first impression that one has is that this is a very clean place.

I'm relaxing in my room after having spent the better part of the morning next door at the health club, Jasmine. It's a women-only day spa, with massage therapy, aerobics, sauna, café, and wonderful showers with hot, hot water. It is just the perfect antidote to two days without a shower, curled up on a plane. The only negative is that there are full-length mirrors and it is hard to avoid noticing how flabby and chubby I've gotten in the stomach, hip, and thigh region. I prefer not to look. I'm trying to reassure myself that I'm off to a good start, if I'm trying to lose a bit of weight — for breakfast I ate raw cucumbers, tomatoes, apples, tangerines, two olives, some sheep-milk cheese and hot tea.

Actually, that sounds like a lot. I think my eating patterns have become a problem. I'm somewhat reassured by the thought that here in Azerbaijan, very few food items have been prepared with preservatives and additives, primarily because of the lack of technology and investment in food processing.

I think that something is definitely wrong with American food. It is shot full of chemicals and additives. No wonder that all American women look like water buffalo. Good grief — I hope that is not my destiny. I do not want to become an American girl water buffalo, or "lady yak."

The water was warm. Hot showers! Beautiful! Who knows when I'll have a hot shower again or be able to dry my hair with an electric blow-dryer.

Time to go downstairs and wait for the ride to Ganja. Checklist for the road: Toilet paper. Azeri currency. Camera. Did I forget my sunglasses? Probably. I hope it's not too cold in Ganja. I hope they have electricity. This reminds me of camping out while doing field investigations in geology. There's a reason I am no longer a practicing geologist, active in the field. I hate camping out, being dirty, cold, and in the dark with nothing to do but stare into a kerosene lantern or campfire and long for alcohol to drink myself into a stupor.

Here's the guy to pick me up. His name is Rufan. It's a six hour drive. Here we go!

All best,
S

March 9
Ganja, Azerbaijan

D:

I forgot to tell you that yesterday was Women's Day. In the Former Soviet Union, that's a big deal. At least it was a big deal for the "real" women. As an American woman, it wasn't much. But the Azeri women got silk flowers, real flowers, and they had a cake and drank champagne. They also got the day off. Guys made elaborate toasts "to the women" and people smiled and said "Happy Women's Day."

"What's that?" I ask.

"Why, it is International Day of the Woman. Don't you have that in America?" they ask.

"No." I say this in an assertive manner, but no one believes me. They look at me with suspicion, as though I am trying to subvert, undermine, or diminish a sacred trust.

"Really, we don't," I continue. Finally, just to stop the indignant looks, I improvise. "But we do have Mother's Day! Yes, I guess we DO have your holiday — I just confused myself because the name is different."

I guess the International Day of the Woman is a deeply emotional holiday for many of the world's peoples. I even got an e-mail from my erstwhile Byelo-Russian boyfriend — the one who is too lazy / indifferent to ever drive across town to see me, but if I want to see him, I have to drive to his dingy, horrible apartment in one of those houses near campus they've converted into apartments. I'm always afraid I'll run into one of my students, although it's not likely, now that I'm not teaching anything but courses via the Internet. In a rare gesture of generosity, he sent me an e-mail. I guess it didn't cost him anything. I shouldn't be so cruel. I supposed I'm still feeling bitter about being exploited, and I still think he panders to me because I occasionally get him high-paying jobs. Maybe not. I don't know. All I know is that I feel sad. Really, deeply sad. I really don't know why I endure this.

What is it about hopeless situations? Why are they so addicting? To me, there is nothing so fascinating (and impossible to tear myself away from) than a good game of "pound the square peg into the round hole." No matter how hard I try, or for how long, the game always seems fresh and new to me. I never seem to tire of the unnecessary and utterly wasteful expenditure of energy that it seems to require. It's so repetitive. I am reminded of a rat or a hamster or a gerbil on a little exercise wheel going around and around and around — finally falling off the wheel after exhausting itself in its run to nowhere.

The problem is, useless effort is time on the hamster wheel — treadmill time that amounts to nothing. But, real time is linear — life time is linear. We get older as we do the empty repetitive things that amount to nothing. How painful is that? Well, the awareness of that is just enough to precipitate in me a big round of anxiety, provoking me to hop right back onto the hamster wheel for a good round of useless spinning.

And that's the way it is with my Byelo-Russian boyfriend. How can I even call him a boyfriend? Perhaps we see each other once a week, but most of the time it is less. He has a tightly-controlled, vaguely agoraphobic life. We have nothing in common except a diffuse sadness about life, a hazy awareness that we haven't quite lived up to expectations. He was supposed to be some sort of big shot intellectual in the capital city. But then the system collapsed.

He struck out for America on a tourist visa. He overstayed. He got asylum. Now he's worried because his friend who came with him has started to leave threatening messages on his answering machine saying that he has turned him into the immigration officials for document fraud. I don't know what this means, but I suppose it is just a matter of time. He will be deported. So, again, he failed to live up to expectations and become a big shot academic in America. Actually, he only rarely goes to school. He's been here eight years, more than enough time to get some sort of degree. And now he's almost 40 years old, never married, no children, and absolutely no way to support children even if he had them. But, he says his parents would love for him to have a child.

Yes, I'm sad because I, too, have failed to live up to expectations. It's relaxing to be with him. But, ultimately, it's not satisfying. How can it be? We can offer each other so little.

But it was still very touching that he sent me an e-mail for International Day of the Woman.

I am angry with myself for feeling so tearful and sad. My life seems so hollow, and all the things that look so solid and attractive on the outside, are, when probed, essentially empty. Such is the case with my relationship with my son, such is the case with my job, with my sense of self. And so, looking at the emptiness makes me feel edgy, restless, filled with angst, and so I plunge into another mindless activity to distance myself from too much introspection.

In the end, will I conclude that my life amounted to just that, and that alone? A frenzy of activity in order to distance myself from my feelings of fear, sadness, loneliness, and failure? And, in doing so, did I distance myself from any of that? Absolutely not. I exhausted myself. I moved my legs. My thoughts spun endlessly. And then, the lack of real spiritual progress was measured in hours, days, weeks, months, years.

That's all I have in common with my Byelo-Russian boyfriend. We are not, in reality, helping each other or ourselves vault over our fears and into a new sphere of success and self-confidence. He is jealous of me. I am resentful of him. I want us to travel into a new dimension of dreams and wishes. I want us to vindicate ourselves in the face of those superimposed "great expectations."

But it's an adolescent fantasy of both separating from and pleasing a rigid parent. Past a certain point, why bother?

And, sadly enough, that's what I feel about love. Why bother?

I'm hoping something will occur to help me at least guess at a reason.

Cheers,
S

ON MATERNAL PANIC, OR ON SADNESS ONCE THE ANGER FADES AWAY

March 9
Ganja, Azerbaijan

Dear Marshall,

I just wanted to write you a letter to tell you how proud I am of you. You are the best son any mother could hope for, and any time that I've been frustrated, it is not because of you, but more about my own frustrations and fears.

How could I have improved things? I wish I could go back in time and do a lot of things over. I still haven't forgiven myself for having married — and I hate myself for what that episode did to you.

I also wish I had never worked in Shawnee at night. It still tears me up that you were all alone at night (your dad was working with the band), and there I was, an hour away, teaching at night. I was glad I quit — and I loved that summer we drove to Shawnee together and you took the Spanish class I was teaching at the university there. I loved the two-hour drive to and from Shawnee with you. Do you remember listening to the radio about the 50-year anniversary of the Roswell, New Mexico "alien sightings?" It was fun to imagine aliens from outer space crashing into the New Mexico desert, and then to think of the government doing experiments with the alien spacecraft.

I also treasure all trips we took together, and the times we spent together. When we went to Arizona, it was great — first when we stayed at Aunt Tek's house. We had so much fun going to different places — do you remember the observatory we went to? Do you remember driving up to Kitt Peak and looking through the huge telescopes? And then we went there in August several years later. Do you remember when we drove through the desert to Tombstone and saw the OK Corral? Then, when we went to Seattle and went to the rain forest and watched the seals and sea otters play — that was fun. And then, the trip to San Francisco when we went on the ferry to Sausalito and were really close to the Golden Gate Bridge? I'll always remember those times — those are the times that I will always treasure.

I wish I had been more of a "normal" mom — and I wish I could go back and spend that time again — this time with you.

It's the truth that you are the only thing in my life that has any meaning.

I miss you very much, and I hope things are going well. Good luck with work, school, friends, & your car. I hope Sammy is okay! Be sure to feed him and to pay attention to him.

Dogs need attention, and especially beagles. I'll never forget the time I was gone for three weeks and Sammy thought I had abandoned him. His tail was all droopy and sad. It was terrible.

I've been doing a lot of thinking while I've been here in Azerbaijan. Actually, there's not much else to do at night — the electricity only works from 7 to 9 p.m., and after that there's nothing to do except sit around and be cold. The heating is electric, too. So, it's around 50 degrees inside.

I'll try to be a better mom. I keep wishing things could have been perfect — that we could have been a perfect family (no divorce, no long trips, no marriage mistakes, no weird freaking out), and I wish I could have been a better mother.

There were just so many things that I thought were silly which actually DID matter. I never thought it mattered about cooking a balanced meal for dinner. It did matter — now your stomach is all torn up because I didn't train you to eat nutritious meals.

I never thought it mattered to take you to church. Now I realize it did and does matter — everyone needs to learn about God's unconditional love, and about values in this world.

I never thought it mattered to have a Christmas tree, or to do all the holidays (decorated, etc.). Now I realize it does matter — those were special time where we could have had nice family outings, family pictures, etc. — and we didn't do it.

And now I wonder why on earth I thought it would be a good idea to read Rabelais to you when you were seven or eight. What was I thinking??? Your teachers thought it was very odd when you repeated some of Gargantua and Pantagruel's stories. It was so much fun to read them to you, though (!). Do you remember how much we both laughed when we read the chapter on "Gargantua Searches for the Perfect Ass-Wipe"?

Good grief. I have been so self-deluding all these years. I hope you can forgive me.

Anyway, I just want you to know that you have a mother who loves you very much, and who will do her best to not let you down. I will always be your mom, and I'd like you to be happy and to have an interesting life.

Much love from
Your MOM

March 11
Ganja, Azerbaijan

D:

I'm staying in a huge remodeled hotel positioned across the street from the governmental buildings. The smell of varnish is making me a bit dizzy. It's a lot better than most Soviet-era hotels I've stayed in. Most are simply bad, like the one in Atyrau, Kazakhstan, which had one thin blanket and a pillowcase with cigarette ashes on it, and NO HEAT although it was almost freezing. This one is warm (delightfully so!), and the paint is shiny, the carpet is new, the floors swept, the staff pleasant (although aggressive about documents).

Right now, I'm in the almost impossibly elegant hotel restaurant. I'm the only woman in sight. There are about 12 tables of men. All men. Aren't they a bit bored? Don't they find the company of women pleasant? Don't they like that exciting interchange of words and chemistry?

I suppose not.

I also suppose that if I were an Azeri woman, my unaccompanied presence would be considered scandalous. But, I'm so obviously a foreigner, I guess I can get away with more things than the local women. I don't want to explore the limits, though. I do not think I will venture out into the night, no matter how bored I may feel. I don't want to arouse suspicion or...

I was interrupted for a moment. The lights went out. Actually, all the electricity went out. It was the third time since I took a seat at this elegantly appointed table, draped with a pristine tablecloth. My room, just one floor up, has a flashlight. Perhaps I should have brought it with me.

Another group of men just came in. Again, no women. I'm looking more closely at the decor. It is very Russian, and I have to say I like it very much. Dark blue walls, white trim, gorgeous parquet floor, intricate silverware, and plates with a delicate pink rose pattern. The lights are refracted through the crystals of ornate chandeliers, and the curtains are a dramatic red velvet. I think of St. Petersburg.

I am not hungry for dinner, mainly curious. So, I order coffee and cake. No cake. So, they deliver chocolates. They are pieces of a sliced Snickers bar. If this were not Ganja, Azerbaijan, I would find that to be a bit presumptuous. I will say that the young waiter served up the sliced candy bar with a great deal of grace and elan.

The waiter, quite young, seems eager to practice English. He can speak it, but not understand it, so I speak to him in Russian. I mention to him that I work with computers, and he explains that there are two Internet clubs in Ganja. He wants to continue talking. I feel pressured. No problem. I am disappearing quickly enough. I have learned not to follow up with these things, because, although everyone is quiet and respectable, inevitably people start believing I can do more than I can. I can't find scholarships or free trips to the US. Actually, if the truth were told, I have once or twice, but those were special circumstances.

This is one of the hazards of traveling alone. Waiters like to strike up conversations. I suppose I look decent. At least I hope so. I look around again. I think I must revise that last statement. I am sure I look a bit scary to most of the men. I'm dressed quite mannishly as Azeri standards go. I'm wearing a black jacket with sailor collar, burgundy knit top, black wool pants, clunky black thick-soled Italian leather shoes, black pearl earrings and a bead necklace. Perhaps the waiter has been sent to me to make sure I'm not some sort of prostitute. Actually, that notion is pretty absurd.

Now I'm back in my room. This is elegant, too. It is a suite of rooms with high ceilings, french doors, lace curtains, mahogany furniture, a spotless and huge bathroom with pillar sink, claw-foot tub, and marble tiles. There is a large bedroom, separate sitting room, entry room, and of course, the bathroom.

I will not tell anyone at home about this hotel. They do not need to know that my experience is at all comfortable. They need to think of me as shivering in the cold, dark night in a refugee tent city, as my face cracks from the dry cold and my dark roots emerge to spoil the bleached blonde halo of hair about my head.

And, it's only $27 per night. That will change once all the construction crews move in for the pipeline.

There are advantages. There are clean, soft sheets, soft blankets, and a nice heater. The only annoyance is the pillow, which is huge and heavy in the Russian manner. One could use it to anchor a boat. One could never use it in one of those 50s movies that featured teenage girls having "pillow fights." One of these pillows would break a neck or snap a spine.

The electricity has gone out again. It is dark and silent outside. I think I will sleep very well tonight.

All best,
S

March 12
Ganja, Azerbaijan

D:

It has been a whirlwind of activity. I spent Thursday and Friday in Barda, a refugee camp two hours from Ganja, and traveled over muddy, rutted asphalt, sometimes two lanes, sometimes one, depending on the depth of the ruts and holes in the roads, and the number of sheep straying into the path of overloaded old Russian Lada cars. We passed through two checkpoints as we went from one region (*rayon*) to another. I tried to imagine how people lived. I saw adobe buildings, concrete block housing and endless clusters of wet sheep, with grayish mud dripping off their skinny haunches. Just as ubiquitous as the sheep were their keepers. A keeper was invariably a dark-jowled man who looked as though he shaved once every third day, slept in his clothing. I knew water and electricity were scarce. I could only imagine the challenge of hygiene.

It's hard to imagine these enigmatic and harsh-appearing men as kind, soft-hearted fathers and friends. Such is the nature of distance and difference.

The cold is not brittle or harsh. It is merely exhausting and inescapable. After awhile, I began to feel feverish from it all. I was chilled to the absolute core, chilled from a damp, wet cold. I was aware that I simply never stopped shivering. Most of the time it was an imperceptible inner shiver, one that exhausted the middle of one's back and upper thighs.

The phenomenology of cold and its effect on the mind and moods is interesting.

The goal was to successfully give a two-day workshop on the basic principles of packaging design and brand image. Most of the refugees were from the occupied Nagorno-Karabakh region, the place where fighting erupted in 1988 (some say as a result of political and economic tensions ignited by perestroika). The war flared up again, then a cease-fire was achieved in 1994. Azerbaijan suffered a severe loss, although it is not clear how Armenia profited by being able to occupy Nagorno-Karabakh.

I remember, back in 1988-89, driving to work as an international operations analyst for Kerr-McGee Chemical Company and listening to Christiane Amanpour reporting from Nagorno-Karabakh. I remember the pronunciation was indeterminate. It changed with every newscast. Little did I know (or imagine), that I would eventually go near there — not just once, but six times in the space of a little more than one year. I remember listening to stories of the one million displaced people — the refugees from Nagorno-Karabakh

— who were living in dire circumstances after being driven from their homes. Little did I know I would be working with them in the future. Strange. Very strange.

Off to the side of the seminar room (which is actually the dining room of a restaurant), is the kitchen. The stoves are heated with wood. The samovars are heated with sticks of wood. Where they get their wood, I have no idea. The mountains around here are barren, with only little clumps of grass for sheep to rip from the dry ground.

I have a throbbing headache. I think it's from dehydration. It could be from despair. I want to understand how we fit into this little world of ours. If only I could have a moment of peace from this terrible anxiety I feel. It would be nice if I could find a couple of Advils.

Yours,
Susan

March 18
Baku, Azerbaijan

Hey Tek,

Here I am, hoping for opportunity, but forced to look inward instead. I returned to Baku yesterday.

For the average American business traveler, the approach into Baku, Azerbaijan, is likely to have an impact like few other places in the world. The Absheron peninsula juts into the southern Caspian Sea like a pale fist, and upon descending one sees immediately that the surface is littered with rusty derricks, slimy, oil-slicked ponds, collapsing factories, unnatural surface impoundments, leaking tank farms, leaking above-ground pipelines, and crumbling worker housing. On the one hand, it brings to mind what great expanses of Oklahoma and Texas might have looked like without oil and gas conservation, spacing requirements, and environmental regulations. On the other hand, it makes one mindful of how close we always are to apocalypse, and all the self-righteous moralizing about saving the environment is somehow moot when faced with either ideological imperatives or the urgent need for resources. Later, the equation becomes more complex when one becomes aware of historical animosities.

Right now, Azerbaijan is more or less racially "pure" — most Armenians, Jews, Russians, and Turks having left for one reason or another. It is a tragic fact that the problems multiplied instead of smoothing themselves out in some great, harmonious promised land. Of course, these issues are not perceptible from the air, but the physical expression of opportunism, repression, resignation, and a no-options-left "fight-to-the-death" focus certainly manifests itself in the gritty breeze that tastes of petrochemicals, and the pervasive smell of natural gas and hydrogen-sulfide-laced oil.

For the average American business traveler, the initial impressions are fairly easy to overlook once one is comfortably ensconced in the Park Hyatt, the newer of the two Hyatt hotels that cater to Westerners. It is almost possible to forget that the Soviet Union looked to the Absheron peninsula, with its twin petro-jewels of oil and natural gas, as an important industrial center. The Absheron peninsula provided the rest of the Union with ethylene, polyethylene, polycarbonates, and a host of petrochemicals. Even after the Siberia oil fields began to reduce the Caspian's hegemony as the world's first oil producer, and expensive secondary recovery was not as attractive as the flush first production of the north, the Absheron peninsula continued to be important.

The Baku Park Hyatt staff members speak English, the television in the room has cable, and all channels with the exception of one from Moscow are in Western European languages. The other exception is the state Azeri station, which tends to replay the same nature / ethnographic documentaries of mountain Azeri villages, accompanied by New Age music by Adiemus or Pat Metheny.

If one has any competency in Russian at all, they will have some opportunities to use it, but not without difficulties. For an American who has learned a smattering of Russian, the Azeri accent is utterly confusing. Russians were the imperial overlords, and even those who were brought in from war-ravaged Ukraine, Poland, and western Russia to build and work in the petrochemical centers, were viewed as privileged.

But, seated in the lounge of the Park Hyatt, drinking a French Bordeaux at $US 15 per glass, snacking on caviar and toast points at $US 28 per person, it is easier to fall into conversations of another sort. Somehow, Baku promotes an ethos of Wild West swaggering and grandiosity, although the evidence contradicts the notion that there exists an infinite and unowned frontier to plunder and skin alive, as in the case of California gold and the Great Plains buffalo.

It's not as easy as it seems — but the fact that President Heydar Aliyev's photograph (or a rug with his image woven in it) hangs in every office or place of business, makes it appear that he's a willing facilitator for Western business. Western grifters looking for a scam hint that they can make things happen. If we can get the President in our pocket, we'll be set, is the unspoken subtext of the grifter's conversation. It is what led to the downfall of the American investors who fell for the pitch of the Czech con artist Victor Kozeny, who claimed to have the president in his pocket. Kozeny said he had access to shares in the soon-to-be-privatized SOCAR, the oil-rich Azerbaijan state oil company.

Kozeny sold shares in privatized industries (vouchers) to the Americans, who thought they'd be able to redeem them for SOCAR. They were wrong. The Azeri government claims Kozeny bilked the Americans on his one dime, and that the $US 90 million he collected from them went into his own pocket. Kozeny claims he paid the Azeri government $US 30 million in bribes, which went directly into offshore bank accounts. The people who worked for Kozeny have another story.

Kozeny's former employees describe "The Bunker" where he kept up to $50 million in cash, along with vouchers and the occasional transshipment of heroin. On one of my trips to Baku, I (supposedly) got to see where The Bunker was. Across the street from some police-related Azeri office, the building housing The Bunker was in an innocuous-looking building, with the sort of inside courtyard that one sees in the buildings near the canals in St. Petersburg.

According to the ex-employees, The Bunker was used for storing cash, vouchers, and packages of heroin in transit from the Iran-bordering Talish region of Azerbaijan to points west. Judging by the number of heroin addicts I saw in St. Petersburg loitering around Kazansky Cathedral across the street from a mafia-run strip club, heroin would probably make its way north as well as west. The only thing that surprised me was that The Bunker was not used for storing forged passports and documents used in alien smuggling. Perhaps that wasn't their specialty. In Paraguay along the Brazilian border, in the Ciudad del Este / Foz do Iguazu region, document trafficking was one of the major industries, with fake passports and documents being Federal Expressed daily to China, and to the Middle East.

I had no idea how the business operated. I had no desire to find out. However, I did observe the ugly impact on the people — the corruption of free will. That is what disheartened me, although it was intriguing to think of oneself as living out a bad spy novel.

I noticed that in Baku, American businessmen were no different than in other places. They suffer from a strange combination of caution and hubris. Both can be fatal. The aversion to risk that characterizes Americans (due to the fact that it is necessary to demonstrate increased shareholder value within a very short period of time — ideally one quarter!) causes them to lose very real investment opportunities and market share which the more aggressive German, Dutch, French, and English pursue at the first opportunity. Perhaps it is due to a difference in overall accounting structure, and how return on investment is calculated. Most Americans want some sort of guarantee. Those who do not are usually of the other category — the absolute antithesis of the cautious accountant types seen before.

Grandiosity is the special purview of the grifter — the type that is most likely to operate on the margins of corporate identity out in the hinterlands where no one can really hold him or her accountable, and where he or she is free to invent and reinvent the Self like a constantly metamorphosing Gatsby. I saw a number of these in Baku — and, strangely enough, many were women.

Straight out of a Jim Thompson noir novel, these women hailed from such exotic locales as Lake Pontchartrain, Louisiana; Port Arthur, Texas; or Lafayette, Louisiana. Utterly lacking formal education, they possessed a surfeit of street smarts and were able to set up restaurants, retail shops, English language schools, job placement services, and all species of businesses they were utterly unqualified to operate. Yet, they pulled it off. After a few years, there they were, dripping diamonds, driving Mercedes, and owners of elaborate townhomes near the center.

Why couldn't I learn to do that?

I guess it's because I think too much.

I'll be back soon. Let's get together and talk about putting together a website.

Love,
Susan

March 22
Baku, Azerbaijan

D:

So I had this great idea that jumping over fire for Novruz, the Islamic Spring festival, would be a good idea.

Leave my misdeeds and sins in the fire. Granted, I would have to do a lot of jumping.

One jump for lying to Evgeny (my erstwhile Byelo-Russian boyfriend), and telling him that Marshall was staying with me when he wasn't doing that at all. It was so I wouldn't have to go over and spend time with him. Why didn't I just tell the truth? I guess I was trying to reserve Yuri for the days when I wanted intimacy. Actually, those days don't seem to happen much any more. I wonder what's wrong.

Maybe I need to take estrogen or something.

One jump for being mean-spirited to Bob and being sarcastic, etc. to him. I thought he deserved it. But, I don't think he would have agreed with me. At any rate, I should have had more self-control.

Two jumps for not getting out more and for spending too much time in front of the computer.

One jump for eating junk food instead of fruits and vegetables.

One jump for not exercising enough.

Two jumps for not thinking of diplomatic ways to talk to Marshall.

Three jumps for complaining to Marshall in front of his friends, for howling, "I'm tired of the way you treat me! You just use my house as an apartment! You have to live with your dad!" Then an hour later, being shamed for losing my self-control and being hyper-critical of Marshall when the truth was, I was just feeling guilty for not spending more time with him.

Ten jumps for being a bad mom and for letting Marshall eat junk food.

About 100 jumps for marrying Zuller, and, once I was smart enough to get out of it, for getting into a sick, twisted, obsessive love thing with him for more than a year (April 95 -September 96). Hmm. I think I'm being too critical of myself. Who could have resisted? It was exciting, adrenaline-charged sex.

One mini-jump for lying to everyone (almost everyone) and for pretending that the five-month marriage never happened and that I was married only once, to Marshall's dad.

Okay. More jumps? One jump for not standing up for myself and for mocking myself. Two (or two HUNDRED) for not telling people that "diversity" is more than just ethnicity, gender, age, or nationality.

It's also about "difference" of any kind — and when my boss talks behind my back to my sister and says that my "problem" is that I have "too many interests" well, I should stand up for myself! I should march right in and argue with him and demonstrate that my chaotic life is actually a benefit for the organization! (But, then I'll have to explain how and when. That won't be so easy to do. Hmmm. Bad strategy.)

Wow. I certainly am defensive.

Two jumps for being overly defensive.

One-half (or micro-jump) for hating the town where I grew up because I let people make me feel bad about myself for being from a small, isolated town near a small, isolated regional center in the middle of a state that is one of the poorest and most miserable in the US. But, being an American in and of itself means that I'm rich, powerful and that I look and live like a movie star.

Five jumps for being a self-deluding narcissist.

By my own calculations, I needed to make approximately 173-1/2 jumps. After that, I'd have a clean slate.

What happens to people who fall into the fire? Will being physically burned up take care of my spiritual garbage? Surely a third-degree burn will count for something.

I, myself, will only jump over the small fires.

Cheers,
S

March 27
in Norman — back from Azerbaijan

D:

We are making our way slowly through the Caucacus Mountains, angling around hairpin curves and trying to avoid the crush of little boys running up to sell green barley sprout bouquets for Novruz. Every quarter mile was another outdoor *chai-hana* — a little tea house, with big brass samovar propped over a fire from sticks. Where they got the sticks, I have no clue. The mountains were denuded of timber. In front of each little *chai-hana* was a little plastic table with flowered oilcloth, a bottle of something, and a grass bouquet in the center. There was no way to determine what was actually in the bottle. Bottles were regularly emptied and filled with something else. That is one symptom of life in a country that has been flattened by change. I think it is a less wasteful way to live. It is good to be ecologically responsible. It is good to recycle.

Good grief, I'm lonely.

I don't know why. Do you ever feel this way? I just have a strange sinking feeling in the pit of my stomach. Should I get up and fight it? Shout out the window? Write angry lyrics, which I will forget? Angry images? Draw, draw, draw — try to turn the sadness into anger, and anger into pain. Pain is easier to manage than sadness.

Okay. So I was searching for medicinal herbs, and someone told me that you could find them along the road — women would be selling them.

I wanted to find herbs for an infusion, something to take away my heart-pain.

I imagine what it is like to hike in beautiful mountains — the Alps or the Rockies. These are barren, and in their barrenness, they are starkly beautiful. There are no trees, just little sheep trails, and green grass with tiny purple blossoms making everything seem like a carpet.

Here are some women. They're standing along a bend in the road, and there are tables set out with piles of plastic bags, and bunches of flowers. The women are dressed in traditional Islamic style — no veils, but headscarves and long skirts. They are holding out clear plastic packets filled with herbs. I recognized rose petals, but nothing else. I bought about ten bags, each a different herb with a distinct medicinal value. The entire lot cost me $1.80. Interesting. The rose petals alone would be something around $15.00 in the US at a boutique store such as the Unique Marketplace around the corner from my house.

I wonder if I'm feeling a bit down because of the general situation in Ganja. A few days ago I noticed that it took awhile to get to the office — the road was blocked by a big tent.

"What's that?" I asked.

There was an awkward pause.

"It's very sad," said Rufan.

"Yeah. We're going to have to walk around the block and it's raining! Is it a little bazaar?" I asked. I thought I was being funny.

"No — oh no!" hushed silence. "It will be here for ten days — someone in the family died."

"I'm so sorry — I had no idea," I said. I looked at the tent constructed in the middle of a fairly busy thoroughfare. I thought I understood. It was a wake. I wondered where the poor deceased family member was. I thought it was a rule to bury the dead within 24 hours.

"What is inside. . . ?" I asked, hesitantly.

"Tea. Coffee. Things for the family. People visit and talk about their memories of the person who has died," explained Rufan.

"Wow. That's interesting," I said.

And the tent was indeed there for several days. And, every time I passed it, I was reminded of my family far away, my aging parents, my aunts and uncles who had died in the last year or so.

It was not very pleasant to be reminded of mortality — my own and that of my loved ones. You only live one time, at least as we are conscious of it. And time slips away.

The road to Baku is dusty and exhaust fumes are creeping into the Russian jeep. I have a headache, and I am wishing there were an Internet connection or work I could do in order to keep from thinking so much. Even a shopping mall would be welcome at this point — anything to keep my mind off the reality of poverty, death, loss, and hopelessness.

I think I'll try to sleep late tomorrow morning.

All best,
S

April 2
Norman, Oklahoma

To the Hungarian (I think) Guy I Saw Last Year on the Flight from Atyrau, Kazakhstan to Budapest.

D:

I have no idea what your name is, who you are, or where you might be. I also realize that there is virtually no chance that I will ever see you again, and that I have no possibilities of finding you.

And yet, I really need and want to contact you. How sad that it is utterly impossible.

I saw you almost a year ago. I was waiting in the departure lounge of the Atyrau, Kazakhstan airport. It was my first trip to Kazakhstan, but not my first encounter with the Caspian Sea.

Kazakhstan reminded me of the western US state of Nevada in more ways than one. For one thing, it was the place where the government tested atomic bombs. For another, it was a place where plutonium fuel rods were stored after being used. And, the landscape was barren — desert, with mountains, dust storms, and a blistering heat that scorched one, even in late April. Oil had been discovered, and there were numerous operations. It was the one thing that attracted large companies such as Chevron, BP-Amoco, and Philips Petroleum to that region.

As we drove toward the airport, I watched two-humped Bactrian camels wander around the shores of the Caspian Sea.

That part was not at all like Nevada. No camels there. Just wild horses and skinny brown rabbits the size of dogs.

When I saw you, I had just finished explaining to the airport officials that I could not possibly pay the $US 100 fine (bribe) they wanted me to pay for having an overweight suitcase. I said that all I had was $US 10. I was sorry, but that was all unless they accepted credit cards. The uniformed woman took my crumpled $10 bill with extreme disgust. "*Stari dolarov*!" (old dollars!) But, she put the all-important stamp in my passport, and I was on my way back to the departure lounge.

And there I saw you. You were adorable, beautiful, radiant. You were seated with a group of five other guys — none of you looked Kazakh or Russian (not that I'm any sort of expert). The relief and joy on your faces was palpable. We were waiting for the same plane — on our way to Budapest on Kazakh Airways.

I kept thinking that I might go over and start up a conversation with your group, but a Bulgarian guy started up a conversation. He kept telling me how relieved he was to be going back home — he had spent nine weeks in Atyrau setting up software for a new branch of ABN-AMRO Bank. Living conditions sounded grim in the extreme. He described how people threw rotting trash into the basements of their apartment buildings, and that there were huge rats. He said that in his apartment building there was no water except for boiling hot water. "Boiling water in a toilet! Can you imagine?" he asked me. "It was disgusting."

I kept looking at you — and I don't know if you realized you had captivated me so much. I don't really know what it was about you — your blonde hair was pulled back into a ponytail, you were wearing overalls, your slender, tall body seemed muscular, but I couldn't really tell. Of course, I didn't let myself stare, slack-jawed with imbecilic admiration. Was it lust? Okay, probably. But there was something about your face — it was gentle, kind, humorous. Your smile was beatific. Your lips soft and gentle, your eyes clear and warm.

What would we talk about? I don't know. What would we do? Chances are, you don't speak English. My Russian is very limited. I think you are probably Hungarian. If so, I speak absolutely no Hungarian. Actually, I did manage to learn the word for "water," but that was all.

There was something about you that seemed wonderfully Central European — urban, kind, warm, down-to-earth.

You seemed to possess all the qualities I like about my Byelo-Russian boyfriend, but none of the negatives. Unfortunately, in his case I think that living in the US has twisted him. He likes to make nasty comments about how I'm a rich, spoiled, and infinitely lucky American who lives in the wealthy part of town, while he has to live like a rat in a one-bedroom apartment in an old house which has been carved into dwellings for the poor and unfortunate (the graduate students at the university) of our town. I really hate it when he says that. True, life is hard, but he has made certain choices. I'm also tired of paying for everything.

There you have it. I saw you, wanted to talk to you, wanted to meet you, but it didn't happen.

I want to apologize to you for lacking the courage to break away from the Bulgarian guy, and for not speaking to you. I apologize for my lack of courage.

Once we arrived in the airport in Budapest, I looked for you, but by the time I made it through immigration, you were gone.

I was stuck in a taxi in a ridiculous situation in which the taxi driver tried to insist that I stay in some place called "Swing

City" and when I explained to him that my business would never reimburse me for a stay in a hotel of that name because in English it gives the impression of being filled with prostitutes and kinky sex, he suddenly pretended to not speak English. I tried explaining in Russian, and then in Spanish. I finally had to hail another cab from the curb outside "Swing City," hoping the entire time that anyone seeing me would realize that at 42 years of age, I was about 25 years over the hill to be any sort of prostitute. To be utterly honest, if anyone had mistaken me for a prostitute, I would probably have been flattered. But, thank God, it was ten in the morning, not ten at night, and no one was desperate enough to think I might be hailing a client & not a taxi.

And, if only I had caught up with you! If only I had enough courage to talk to you! We could have walked around Budapest, sat at an outdoor café and talked about life. If we couldn't communicate, I suppose we could at least drink heavily.

And then you could have come back home with me. We could stop at home long enough for me to introduce you to my family, for me to quit my job, buy tickets back to Europe, and for us to have long, romantic nights as we looked at the stars and talked about life, love, thoughts, and the nature of perception. I'm assuming that my command of Hungarian would have increased at a superhuman pace. I could have introduced you to my son, who would, by that time, be comfortable with his father, have entered the university at an early point, and be earning more money than the combined income of his father and myself, thanks to his computer skills.

And then, you and I could have had long, torrid nights of sex, sex, and more sex, as I tried to ignore the fact that on April 2 (today, in fact), I would turn 43.

We could have spent six glorious months wandering around Central Europe before I would have been forced (by pride, dignity, and female vanity) to disappear on a plane back to nowhere before my breasts started to sag and my belly became flabby without my grueling routine of aerobics classes and swimming.

Hmm. To tell the truth, this pragmatic look at likely outcomes is not very appealing. It's not sounding very romantic. It's probably just as well that you will never receive this letter.

But, still I think about you almost every day, and my daydreams are filled with images of you, your kind eyes and gentle smile.

Today is my birthday. I offer you champagne, a nice little birthday dinner, a wish for your well-being and good fortune. I don't know your name, but I offer you all the good I have inside me to make your life better, to comfort you when you are sad and lonely, to assuage your fears, and to hold you when the nights are long, dark, and cold.

With my love, I send this letter and a kiss,

Susan

April 16
Norman, Oklahoma

Hi Tek,

Well. Here it is. It is "Tax Day." Officially, yesterday was, but since yesterday was Easter, it was changed to today. The lines are long at the post office, and people around work are grumbling about it. But, I'm not worried about it. I'm getting money back this year because too much was deducted from my paycheck. What will I do with the money? I think I'll try to save it.

Did you go to church for Easter? I didn't have any intentions to go (too crowded, don't know where to go, etc.), then Dad called and asked me when / where I would go. I said, well, I don't think I'm going, plus I want to be here in case Marshall needs me. He is extremely sick — still has a fever, terrible sore throat, and is absolutely exhausted. I took him to the Minor Emergency Clinic on Saturday and they said he had "mono" — and that it can be dangerous because if there are any activities such as contact sports (or skateboarding), the spleen can rupture.

That made the hair on the back of my head absolutely stand on end. Marshall went skateboarding a few days ago because he started to feel a little better. Then, he came home barely able to stand up due to the extreme pain in his side. Good grief! He could have ruptured his spleen! He is really miserable, and can barely swallow anything. I've been getting him ice cream, ice cream shakes — anything to help him drink liquids. The doctor told me to make an appointment with Marshall's regular pediatrician as soon as possible and to avoid dehydration since that's what usually leads to hospitalization. Of course, a ruptured spleen would lead to a bad situation, too.

Anyway, Dad said that "God wants you to go to church. It is HIS day." Then, I started having horribly guilty and fearful feelings — if I didn't go to church on Easter, would God punish me? Would He refuse to let Marshall heal, just to punish me? Would He refuse to let Aunt Jorena get out of intensive care where she's been since she had a cardiac problem after breaking her shoulder in her home in Dallas? Would He swoop down like an enormous bird of prey and torture me just as a demonstration of omnipotence and whimsy? Oh no, that's Zeus and Ganymede. I confused the two.

I don't like to think of God as a sadistic despot. Unfortunately, I don't have much of a conception of God at all. I have read biblical texts, and I have attended church, but my idea remains rather chaotic. Is God a tribute-demanding tyrant? Is God an omniscient and inescapable stalker? Is God an indifferent clockmaker who, only occasionally, looks down upon His creation and winds the clock so that the inevitable cause-and-effect relations will continue to play themselves out?

Although Dad was putting on the pressure, I resisted. I didn't go. I told him I felt uncomfortable. Later that afternoon, I called him up and said that I didn't really like the emotional blackmail element, and it made me feel cornered and incapable of living up to people's standards. Actually, if you think about it, that statement was absurd. It wasn't impossible to live up to other people's standards — all I had to do was to throw myself in the shower, put on decent clothing, and brave the unknown (and the social pressure). How different is that from work?

"Don't worry. If Marshall is that sick, you could be a carrier. It could be dangerous and irresponsible for you to go to church, where you could infect older people who have no resistances," said Dad.

Strangely enough, instead of feeling relieved, I felt worse. Unclean! Unclean!

But, it was easier that way. As an official "carrier" of the Epstein-Barr virus, I can be as lazy and irresponsible as I want (joke).

If I think about it, the concept of God I prefer is that of "God is Perfect Love." In other words, God is the name we give to the originator of all positive energy in the world — all transcendent mental energy, all those times when the physical and the intellectual converge. If one understands how God Is Love works, then one can develop the mental discipline to transform oneself and to become a better, kinder, more enlightened being. One can begin to feel compassion and to empathize with the situations of others. This must occur through the transformation of one's thoughts.

This sounds suspiciously like Buddhism. That's okay by me.

Love from,
Susan

18 April
Norman, Oklahoma

D:

What a week so far. Gorbachev came to Norman, Marshall's fever lingered, his sore throat and general misery were diagnosed as mono, and I joined a "Fat Club."

Okay. I know I'm not following your advice to be less critical of myself.

But, joining the "Fat Club" is not being hard on myself. I just succumbed after three months of having to look at the hideous sight of DOCTOR'S SCALES in the empty office across the hall from me. The women around the office decided to weigh in each Monday and record their weight on an index card that lists us by the last four digits of our social security number.

Okay. Most of them are pretty fat. I'd say that there are at least 10 women in my building alone (and there are only about 30 in all) who weigh more than 200 pounds. Ghastly! They have bad knees and bad hips. The first thing they do is get a list of birthdays, holidays, special university "holidays," and then they form committees to decide who brings cake, pastries, coffee, soft drinks, and sometimes an entire lunch. It's crazy. The office desks groan under the weight of so much food. In one office, three secretaries sit up front. I always think of women being interred alive behind a wall — this time, it's a wall of donuts, cakes, pastries, and Wapanucka's famous homemade Frito Chili Pie Lasagna.

Well, I'm always attracted to a handout and free food, so this has been a dangerous environment for me. Over the last few years, I haven't gained too much weight, but I feel myself slipping out of control. (To tell the truth, I like that adrenaline rush — out of control . . . !) So, I joined the health club & tonight was my first night at aerobics. It was okay. I hadn't been in about four years, and aerobics has changed a lot. I think I'll go again tomorrow, but just hang out on one of the exercise bicycles.

It's the health club at Brookhaven Village — just down from Crispy's. Was it there when you lived here? I think it was. I always thought it must be an expensive, upscale place. Actually, it's not. It's crowded with weight machines, exercise bicycles, stair-climbing machines, etc., and it has a fairly gritty, utilitarian feel to it. What I like about it is that it's a three-minute drive from the house, or, if it's not dark, a 10-minute walk.

I wonder if I should try diuretics? Maybe one of those all-grapefruit diets? (Joke.)

Have you been doing any health / diet things lately? I remember you got really thin at one point. I think you were having migraines due to all the pollen and dust in the air, and you were fasting / starving yourself until it went away. You also walked a lot, which I always thought was cool.

I do have regrets that you and I never hooked up. I wish we had been able to be together in some sort of permanent bond before you went away.

It is your misanthropic side that I admire. I admire your bitter sense of humor, and your willingness to be direct. You have a fantastic sense of humor, and you are willing to live life exactly as you please. That is inspiring, and I often think about you, and how you might react to a certain thing. It is often good to refuse to do something, and to refuse to buy into the latest self-help and "leadership" prattle.

Our conversations were much more stimulating and meaningful than any I've had since. Although Norman is a university town, there are surprisingly few people who are truly thoughtful and/or contemplative.

I somehow hang on in the weird branch of academia that must be partially entrepreneurial, and partially traditional. Actually, I like it, although it has its rough moments. The snobbishness and elitism, combined with hypocrisy and a thinly-masked atmosphere of pedophilia (in some camps) is rather hideous. Fortunately, I can avoid a lot of that.

I really enjoy our chats about films. I'm still going to try to make it to Elko, but the fact that Marshall is living with me 100% of the time, and that he has mono, are two complicating factors.

Talk to you soon!

All best,
S

18 April
Norman, Oklahoma

Jeffords:

I don't think it's absolutely necessary to write you this letter, but perhaps it's not a bad idea. I don't know.

If Marshall and his dad hadn't had their terrible confrontation, I would have come out to Charleston.

As it turns out, I'm glad I didn't. You're still married! And you said that you were served divorce papers, and the marriage was in essence, over.

Okay. That may be so. But why are you spending Easter weekend with your wife and two daughters?

I still think that what you have is a commuter marriage. You got the gig in Charleston as Human Resources Vice President, you bought a condominium, then you moved. Your wife didn't want to leave her successful business. She didn't want to sell your home. So, the two of you are commuting.

It seems degrading to me to be the "other woman." Plus, why would I want to get between the two of you if there is a chance of a successful marriage?

I can't believe you said "top priority" was for me to move to Charleston. Pray tell, WHY? What would I do there? Sweating in the azaleas and wandering through old slave quarters does not appeal to me. I don't like "Southern Gothic" genres. And, your patronizing crap about how "cute" it is that I like to write poetry would eventually lead to verbal fisticuffs.

Oh, and when you told me that "Even though I'm taking Zoloft for my depression, and can't really perform, I can still give you pleasure," it made my skin crawl. No thank you! How shallow do you think I am? Do you think I would drop everything and move to Charleston to be your love-slave-on-the-side just to observe complete and total sexual dysfunction?

As usual, I find myself asking the old, familiar question: "Is there anything AT ALL in this for me?"

As usual, the answer is "ABSOLUTELY NOTHING" — except for the "anthropological experiment" potential. But, I've done that one all too many times.

I've been home when you called. I just refuse to answer. I have decided to try to act as though I possessed self-esteem. What do they say? "Fake it until you make it."

Right now, I'm faking being self-righteous, morally correct, and happy. Maybe someday soon I'll make it to that point.

Happy Easter with your Wife and Kids,
— Susan

April 24
Norman, OK

Hey Tek,

I really like the draft of the website you've put up. I think we need to include something about the two wildcats we have planned.

To be realistic, they'd have to be called "rank wildcats." High risk exploratory wells, more than one mile from existing oil and gas production. Way out there. We're "elephant hunting" and searching for something significant. We need something good.

It's the theme of my life these days. Searching, that is. Love, companionship, a formula for being a good mom, jobs, investment opportunities, trinkets to import and sell in the gift shop, an effective diet and exercise plan, etc..

If I find what I'm looking for, what will I do? Will I even be able to recognize it?

The well we have planned is near Asher, Oklahoma. It's fairly remote. There are no major highways, and bridges across the Canadian River are few and far between. We've leased a total of 1,280 acres, which total two full sections. If the entire leased area is productive, we could have as many 32 wells, on 40-acre spacing. If the wells average 100 barrels per day production, that could mean 3,200 barrels per day. You can do the math — if oil averages $20 per barrel, and we have 75% net revenue interest — well, we'll be in tall cotton, high clover, in the money! I think we can drill and complete each well for around $350,000 per well. There will be operating costs, of course, but if we average 100 barrels per day, we can cover a lot of costs.

That's the best-case scenario, of course. The worst-case scenario is that it's a dry hole, and we lose $250,000. Talk about gambling.

This afternoon, I'm going to meet with Claudine Stufflebean. Yes, that's really her name! She's the owner of the surface, but she doesn't own any of the minerals. I need to come to some sort of surface damage settlement. Usually we pay $2,500. In her case, I'm going to see if she'll take $1,000, and we'll gravel the turnaround drive near her barn, replace her cattleguard, and asphalt the driveway near her house. It's worth a lot more than $2,500, but it doesn't cost us that much because we do a lot of this stuff and we can get a good deal.

She lives out in the country in an old farmhouse that was built in the 1920s. It is a two-story wood-frame house, with large windows, big cottonwood trees that provide lots of shade in the summer, and lots of mess in the spring and fall. When you go inside, you feel as though you've gone back in time. The furniture is unchanged from 50 years ago, and the house usually smells of pecan pie or biscuits. She's around 70. Her daughters live in California, and her grandchildren are scattered over the US.

No one in her family seemed to want to stick around Oklahoma. Well, who can blame them. We're part of that great depopulating swath of country that extends throughout the Great Plains.

Imagine living in an enormous ghost town. That pretty much describes us here in Oklahoma.

It's ironic, isn't it? I am a person who hates gambling. I like Lady Luck, but I like it to be a presence that rewards hard work, not Russian Roulette-type all-or-nothing activities.

Claudine has a telephone. No computer, no internet, no fax, no cell phone. Is she happier for it? Her comfort zone is well-defined and, at her stage in life, there is little or nothing to disturb it.

I hope she has baked a pecan pie. I'm hungry. Hope you can go with me.

Love,
Susan

April 25
Asher, Oklahoma

D:

I used to take Marshall fossil hunting not far south of here, in the Arbuckle Mountains. After we'd look for fossils, we'd go on a tour of small towns listed in a travel book, GHOST TOWNS OF OKLAHOMA. It was a lot of fun. It described the boom-bust cycle of the coal-mining towns and late 19th-century oil settlements, such as Petrolia, now long abandoned. It was fun to read the stories — many were towns settled by the five Indian nations, the Choctaw, Chickasaw, Cherokee, Creek, and Seminoles, who were forced to resettle in Oklahoma after their deadly forced march, the "Trail of Tears."

Right now, we're drilling for oil on land that was once assigned to Pottawatomi Indians, who had resettled from Indiana and Illinois.

Last week, we spudded in, which means that the drill rig moved in and started drilling the mouse hole (or rat hole), whichever term you prefer. That's a hole in the ground where they store the drill pipe. After they completed that, they started to drill the regular hole. The first 1,500 feet were drilled with a wider drill bit because we have to set surface casing in order to protect the aquifer. It's against the law to allow drilling fluids (or any other fluids) to enter the groundwater and contaminate it. We finished setting surface casing last night, and now we're drilling ahead. I'm nervous. We have a lot riding on this well. Not only is it expensive ($250,000 to drill, another $100,000 to complete if we encounter oil), it's also a large prospect. We've leased the equivalent of two full sections. That doesn't sound like much, but it's pretty big for Oklahoma, especially for a well that's fairly shallow. We will TD (reach total depth) at around 5,700 feet.

We can't really afford for this to be completely dry. It's a rank wildcat, which means it's more than a mile from established production. However, the Calvin Sand is widely productive in this area, and I think that we're likely to be able to make a 10-barrel-day well. The Layton is the same, but sometimes it produces gas with the oil. It could be good for 10 barrels / day and 250 MCF (thousand cubic feet) of natural gas per day. Of course it's not the 250 barrels per day we'd like. But, we'll take it. The primary objective, the Wilcox Sand, has produced tremendous amounts of oil — 1,000 barrels per day in the Seminole Field back in the 1920s. Such flow damaged the formation ("coning"), so it's best to choke it back to 100 barrels per day. The pressures are good — it's a water-drive reservoir, and with the 35% porosity that the well-sorted, clean sandstone contains, it can produce for as many as 50 years, if managed correctly.

Last night, as I was sitting in the geologist's trailer, listening to the motors, the mud pump, and the clanking of tongs on pipe as they made a connectio and added another length of drillpipe, I realized that I have this business in my veins. I don't always like the risk. Actually, I never like it. But, I love the idea that by finding oil and gas, we generate wealth that benefits all sorts of people. The state picks up its tab, and excise tax supports all sorts of government programs. The landowners, royalty owners, workers, and small company participants benefit. Fifty years ago or so, Oklahoma was dominated by small producers, although the big boys were here, too. I'm not saying that there weren't robber barons and dishonest sharks. However, the little guy had a chance.

The towns were filled with small businesses, and most were family-owned. It was before the advent of Wal-Mart, Texaco StarMart, McDonald's, Pizza Hut, and all the chains that drove small businesses out, and punished eccentricity and/or creativity. No longer can people own their own businesses, nurture their dreams. They must work for 20 hours per week, with no benefits, until carpal tunnel syndrome causes them to be useless to their employer.

Small oil operations offer a dream of freedom, and a potential escape from the tyranny of the chain.

Too bad you have to be a gambler to do so!

All best,
S

May 2
Asher, Oklahoma

Hey Tek,

This is great. We've made a discovery. Sorry for the disjointed nature of this letter. I've been up all night. We ran logs last night, and I stayed up for the whole thing. I was sure that they would look fairly okay — we had good shows of oil in the Calvin and in the Layton. Both had decent porosity — 18 percent. The Wilcox didn't look too good. Oil stain, but not much. It will depend on how many feet of oil zone there seems to be. We need at least 15.

The logs showed the Wilcox to have four feet of oil-saturation. That's not enough. The Calvin has 20 feet. The Layton, 12. It's a go in those zones. We're going to set pipe.

We can't expect 100 barrels per day. We'll probably get 30 to 40, with some water. That's okay by me! It will pay for the well, cover costs. At least it's not a total loss!

I'm exhausted, but I thought you'd like to know.

Love,
Susan

May 8
Norman, Oklahoma

D:

Do you remember what I said about "letting go" and "giving up the false illusion of control?"

I have decided I was wrong about that. It is a mistake to give up control. What one needs to do is get MORE control. Over one's thoughts. Over one's responses. Over one's mental processes.

My goal, starting NOW is to meditate, do yoga, pray — all so that I can have MORE control over my mind, my nerves, my tendency to be histrionic and to panic. Thus, I will be able to let go and not be worried about the things that occur that are beyond my control.

The mind is a beautiful thing. I can construct my own reality — not so much in the phenomenal world, but at least within the emotional and psychological landscape where I romp about.

How are things in Elko?

I miss you.

Kisses,
S

May 12
Lake Naivasha, Kenya

Dear D:

The light was as cool and clear as the temperature. At 5 p.m. in East Africa, so close to the equator, the sun was already within two hours of setting. Unlike the "White Nights" I had experienced in St. Petersburg, Russia, two years ago, almost to the day, when the sun sets here, it is definitive. Light to dark. It is a darkness that is neither thick nor tropical, but weightless and unguarded, partially because of the altitude and partially because of Kenya itself.

This is a vacation. It's also a chance to attend a seminar, "Future Oil and Gas Concessions in East Africa." Again, I'm trying to see if there are opportunities out there. I would like a company to hire me to help them start up in Kenya and Uganda.

Kenya will probably never be a place or a thing I can define, except in terms of my own awakenings and approach to life. I will always remember this place, and this particular 5 p.m., seated on a pier that extends out into Lake Naivasha, a Rift Valley lake near Nairobi.

The smell of wetlands, and the sound of hippos quietly sliding beneath the waters make my skin tingle. I hear boats approaching the shore, their owners turning off the engines as they reach land. They, too, are dealing with that issue of day vs. night and the pervasive rhythms of dreams and dreaming.

He described his wife to me. I was uninterested, but I knew it would be impolite not to feign some sort of detached compassion. Besides, I had conned him into doing this day-long safari so that we would have the minimum number of participants (2) in order to actually take off. His wife was, according to him, a woman who could put away two bottles of wine every night, but still look like a 25-year-old and play in tennis tournaments while her children were cared for by the *au pair*. Now, instead of feeling mere disinterest, I was feeling vaguely jealous. An *au pair*? Playing tennis all day? The stay-at-home mom who didn't really have to stay at home?

I didn't want my face to show my envy. I tried to maintain a look of bland acceptance. Unfortunately, my mind wandered, and all I could think of were lurid sex fantasies of what could go on in the little cottages lying along the flowering tree-shaded walkways where iguanas darted and colorful birds squawked mellifluously. Mellifluously? Perhaps not. Mellifluous would be the way one's moans of pleasure would harmonize with the sound of hippos submerging themselves into the dark waters.

The heart of Africa was perfumed by jacaranda trees, trumpet lilies, and bright carnations, an exotic blend spiced by the aroma of lake fish and rotting lilypads.

His voice droned on.

Water lapped up against the pier as the wind shifted. The sex fantasy was quickly metamorphosing into a self-pitying narrative as I contemplated the unfairness of it all. How did it happen that I was in such a romantic setting without any opportunity at all for spontaneous misbehavior? I didn't even see any room for the actions of fate or destiny. Oh well, at least I wouldn't have to worry about bulging thighs or unshaven legs.

When my mind finally returned to the scene at hand, he was waiting, expectantly, like a dog sitting for a meat treat. He wanted female affirmation.

"Wow. You've really had it rough," I said. I glanced at him. "But, you've been incredibly successful. You should be proud of yourself for that."

I hoped that what I said had some bearing on whatever it was that he had been telling me.

He nodded fervently and went on. I returned to my unsatisfying sex fantasy. At least we would be eating dinner soon.

He continued to talk. I continued to let my mind drift. Usually I was the one chattering on. Role reversals. Oh well. Travel is like that.

Talk to you soon,
Susan

June 13
Mind somewhere, but not sure where

Dear D:

I got back from Kenya a week ago. I'm still eight hours off schedule. Ahhh — jet-lag. You have to love it! Living on the edge all the time.

You never know what you have to do to take the edge off. I mean, you'd think that with as much travel as I do or have done, I would no longer get travel anxiety. But no, my experience really makes no difference at all. I get travel nerves. I can't seem to avoid them.

I'm hanging out with a friend from Tulsa who raises horses. We're planning to stop in Gainesville and check out the factory outlet mall for "tax free weekend" shopping. We met at the IHOP on Ed Noble Parkway. I don't think it had been built when you lived here. At that time, there was a little farmhouse and a modest stand of cedar trees, and not much else. You and I always met at Denny's. In my opinion, Denny's is better.

I woke up at 5 a.m. — plenty of time to get ready, right? In theory, yes. I did make it to the IHOP by 7:35 a.m.. He was already there, waiting patiently. We ate breakfast and decided to take one vehicle to the train station. I left my car in the parking lot of the adjacent La Quinta hotel. I was secretly hoping that someone would recognize my car in the parking lot and wonder what I might be up to in a motel less than a mile from my house. Weekend job at La Quinta working the front desk? Conducting training? Bumping and grinding in an illicit love affair?

As I was contemplating the crimes of passion I could be potentially suspected of committing, Rob grabbed his backpack and opened it up, pulling out a huge bottle of a rather murky golden liquid. It seemed to foam slightly.

"Here — want some for the road?" he asked. He tried to hand me the bottle. "It's never too early in the day to get started. Take the edge off."

"It's good and old. Jurassic age," he said. I smiled. Sixty million years old was quite old indeed.

"No thanks," I declined. He lifted up the bottle and chugged down five or six swallows.

"Wow," I said. In spite of myself I was impressed. I wondered how he intended to drive. Fortunately, all we had to do was make it to the train station across town. Then some-one else would do the driving.

"Are you sure?" The liquid foamed gently against the glass. I'm not a whiskey connoisseur, but what I saw did not look promising.

"Maybe later. This evening. Maybe. If I drink this early, I'll have a headache." I perceived myself speaking too quickly and nervously. Travel anxiety? Perhaps. Especially with a guy who, by all appearances, would be drunk by 9 a.m..

He chugged a few more swigs.

"It's tea." I looked more closely. The vague turbidity and foaminess were definitely more indicative of tea than of whis-key. Lipton's? Arizona Sun Tea?

This reminded me of my finding two bottles — one of rum, and the other of cheap vodka — in Marshall's room last summer. Both were filled with a liquid that was not alcohol. "It was a joke for Nathan's birthday party," he explained. I saw no humor in it. The bottles had been full at one point or another. The question was, had Marshall and his teenage friends been in possession of the full bottles? I suspected that the answer was yes. Grrr. The old, familiar, helpless-mom feeling was coming back.

I looked at Rob. He was looking at me oddly.

"You're hard to shock," he said, somewhat disappointedly.

"Oh?" My mind was wandering. I had begun to wish that the liquid had, in fact, been whiskey. Something to take the edge off? Good. Keep a bottle in the backpack? Why not.

A year or so ago, I was waiting in the Budapest airport for a charter Russian Tupelov jet to take me and a group of guys to Atyrau, a town located on the northeast edge of the Caspian Sea, where so much drilling is taking place. My fellow passengers were oilfield workers — primarily drilling crews and those who did well and formation fluid testing. All were Scottish with the exception of a guy from Finland.

"Would you like to drink some vodka with me?" he asked, in Russian. Delighted to be able to practice Russian, I responded in Russian with a delighted, "Da. Thank you very much."

Actually, I thought that perhaps he was joking, but he was not. He pulled out a bottle of vodka and poured some into a small plastic cup. He handed it to me.

"Cheers," he said, and drank the shot he had poured himself.

"Bottoms up," I said. I drank mine. It felt nice. It did take the edge off.

The Russian-speaking guy from Finland sat next to me on the plane. I practiced Russian. He gave me his address in Helsinki. Needless to say, I never wrote to him. I might have, perhaps, but I lost his address somewhere along the way.

He had been planning to go out to the well that night, but there were production problems, and his departure was delayed by a day. He spent the night in the new prefabricated Hotel Chagala, which looked like a Motel 6 — where the people I was to work with were staying. I was supposed to stay there, but they were full.

Chagala meant something like Shangri-La, which I found out was most certainly the case when compared to the old Soviet-era hotel where I stayed. Granted, it only cost $10 per day, but still, you'd think you'd get clean sheets and running water for that. Instead, I got a room with a bed that had cigarette ashes on it, one blanket, a dirty sheet, and two big square pillows that must have weighed 10 pounds apiece. Whatever they filled the pillows with, it wasn't goose down. It had the consistency of dirt, and smelled about like that, too. It was so cold that night, though, that the pillows made impromptu insulators to position over the core of my body. Although it was chilly in April, the management had shut off the gas heat "because it was already spring."

I didn't get much sleep, thanks to the Russian disco music that reverberated from the club downstairs. I was thirsty, but the bottled water that the female room attendant in the flowered head scarf had given me was "not for drinking." It was clearly marked for washing. To drink it would mean serious illness.

The next morning, I presented myself at the Hotel Chagala, where my business associates were meeting me for coffee and breakfast. I hoped that my hair did not look too matted, and that my attempts at a sponge bath with the contents of the "for washing" bottle of water were successful.

Seated at the table next to us was my new-found Finnish friend who clearly wanted me to join him. I smiled at him, and greeted him briefly. "Business meeting," I explained briefly. "I hope the job is great and that you have a successful trip."

As I chatted with my associates, my Finnish friend looked at me. His face was sorrowful. With a fingertip, he traced the path of an imaginary tear coursing down from his eye to his jaw. I was appalled and flattered.

I drank my coffee and wondered if there was something that could take the edge off the tension that pervaded the room. The consortium led by Shell had been testing a new discovery, and everyone was eagerly awaiting results.

Later, I found out that the night I arrived was the night the tests came in. They were overwhelmingly positive. We would soon learn that their engineers estimated that the field contained 300 million barrels of oil.

Would my life have been different if I had been able to take the edge off? Could I have secured myself a job working in the newly-discovered giant field? Could I have kept in touch with the Russian-speaking guy from Finland. Was that my last, best chance to find love and fulfillment? Perhaps. I don't know. I can't tell from here. I never did take the edge off.

The edge will always be there when I think of you. I can't help it. My determination to control my emotions was sort of a waste. I cry anyway.

I miss you. You just have no idea —

A big sloppy hug and lots of sloppy kisses (too late, of course, which explains why they're sloppy with tears),
S

June 13
Masai Mara, Kenya via
Somewhere near Pauls Valley, Oklahoma

D:

It's a hot morning, but we have refrigerated air here in the passenger cars in the AMTRAK Heartland Flyer that goes from Oklahoma City to Fort Worth, Texas, with stops in Norman, Purcell, Pauls Valley, Ardmore, and Gainesville (TX).

I'm looking out the window to cornfields, pastures, trees, and bright red earth. There's a stock pond and a couple of guys are fishing. I'm not sure what they'll catch in that hot, muddy, red water. Catfish, perhaps? It's hard to tell. In Paraguay, the local river catfish are called *surubi* and they are considered an aphrodisiac, and c*aldo de surubi* (surubi soup) is supposed to be able to enhance male sexual performance. I'm not sure why. I asked, and got an evasive response about protein content. It makes no sense to me — in Paraguay, men also drink tea made of the bark of the lapacho tree. It's supposed to be a sort of all-natural Viagra. As far as I can tell, it's all about the suggestibility of the morphology of something.

If it looks like a phallus, then it must be good for the phallus. That must be how it goes.

I've never heard anyone say that the red dirt here is good for the heart, although it's red like blood. Actually, the soil is red due to iron oxides in the Garber-Wellington formation which outcrops here. There is a significant amount of clay in the sand which accounts for the turbidity of the water. Red. Red earth. That's what Oklahoma is all about.

We're getting ready to make a stop in Pauls Valley. The town of Pauls Valley is positioned in a bend in the Washita River, which is a fairly narrow, deep, slow-moving, meandering stream. In years past, before they built the dams, the river used to flood and there were periodic outbreaks of malaria.

Supposedly, you can't get malaria these days in Pauls Valley. They say the mosquitoes are under control. In contrast, everyone I met in Kenya had suffered from malaria. I just finished taking anti-malaria medicine last week, and thankfully it worked. I did not contract malaria, as far as I know. Nor did I contract encephalitis, meningitis, yellow fever, or hepatitis. I sometimes have doubts, though — I've been fairly disoriented the last month since returning from Kenya. It may be the shock of getting back into my life. Or, it could be something physical. Who knows? Maybe I'm suffering from some sort of deep depression. All I know is that I have, more than once, felt dizzy and faint while talking. It wasn't unpleasant — just a mild vertigo feeling.

The conductor is announcing that there will be delays on the way to Gainesville. Track repair, he says.

Some of the passengers look a bit alarmed, and express concern that they won't have sufficient time for shopping. The outlet mall is large, but it's not huge — four hours should be more than sufficient time. I have stopped at the mall several times — it's right off the interstate halfway between Norman and Dallas. It's a great place to stop and stretch one's legs. Once I bought books on tape and listened to Roddy McDowell regale the listener with sordid details of Marlene Dietrich's life.

Marshall used to like listening to the tapes. I'll never forget one of those times. We listened to stories of aliens, UFOs and unexplained phenomena as we traveled to Southern Methodist University in Dallas where I was giving a poetry reading.

That was when I had the Infiniti Q45. Did you ever see it? What a beautiful luxury experience — burlwood appointments, leather seats, quartz crystal clock. Elegance and privilege. It was great when it was running and didn't cost me a small fortune to keep on the road.

The conductor is now chiding people for not having purchased tickets ahead of time. "You pay twice as much if you don't have reservations," he says.

Well, that's not really the point. I have so few experiences like this that the money is not an issue. This is not merely transportation. It's an experience.

In Kenya, at the Masai Mara game preserve, one can take an air balloon ride to see the migration of the wildebeests. It's $US 400, if you purchase in advance, through an agent. If you just show up, it's $US 200. So, just the reverse is true in Kenya. I opted not to go for the balloon. I preferred to do a safari by Range Rover. It cost $US 155 per day per person. It was worth every cent, because, as opposed to a balloon ride, in a Range Rover-led game drive, you can stop and park for awhile. It's a great way to see the animals.

I needed the safaris. After days of struggling with grant writing, proposals, making presentations on the virtues of integrated maize/grain information systems, it was a relief to sit back and let someone talk to me about flamingos and hyenas.

Looking down from an overlook into the East African Rift Valley, the first thing that impresses one is the vastness of it all. The rocky cliffs abound with hidden nooks, caves, and hiding places. One can well imagine the lifestyle of the early hominids — protohumans, if you will. It's not too hot, not too cold on the equator at 6,000 ft. elevation. There are lots of fish, birds, fruit, and vegetables. There are, however, venomous snakes, stinging nettles, thorny trees, and bugs of shocking virulence. I am careful not to eat anything unpeeled, uncooked, or unwashed. Do I want to be an open invitation to parasites?

Of course not. Not really. But no matter how careful one is, there is that pesky issue of feelings of invincibility. We're all teenage boys at heart. We think we can fly, and that death is nothing more than a persuasive technique — a tool to use to make people feel bad.

Mortality is an omnipresent issue in Kenya. The obituaries are filled with pictures of young men and women, cut down in their 20s and 30s.

Children die of malaria. Adults die of malaria. Malaria is malaria. It is also a euphemism for AIDS.

No malaria here. That's a relief. I tell myself that to keep myself on the right track. It's nice to be on a train, far away from life's annoyances. I'm listening to snippets of overheard conversation, but I'm thinking less of Oklahoma and tax-free shopping, and more of life, death, sickness, and of the existential shame that comes with the awareness of one's own human condition.

But traveling is supposed to take one away from that, right? We're near the Washita River, as it cuts through the Arbuckle Mountains, elevation 2,000 feet. On the left of the train is a quarry. It looks like one that Marshall and I explored when he was around five years old. We collected fossils from the Devonian Hunton formation, which was just chock-full of brachiopods, cephalopods, trilobites (smaller than the ones I bought in Bolivia), crinoid stems, and gastropods. It was also a denning area for rattlesnakes, which I found out later as we stopped by the nature center at Chickasaw National Park. That wasn't pleasant!

On the right, over a bank, is the river. A man in waders is fishing in the rapids. The water is muddy, but it is less red here than brown. Now we're in a grove of trees. I see horses, rusty trailer homes, abandoned tires, and other signs of rural poverty. It doesn't look too unpleasant — at least from here. But then, the poisonous thorn trees in Africa looked pretty — from a distance.

That's what you said about me once.

I need to talk to you. I'll be sending you lots of positive thoughts.

Warmest,
Susan

ON STRANGE LITTLE REPETITIONS, OR YET ONE MORE RIDE ON THE GREAT HAMSTER-WHEEL OF LIFE

7 July
Norman, Oklahoma

Hey Tek:

My life makes no sense at all! You're not going to believe this — I was sitting in my office this morning, waiting for the carpet guys to come in and take out my furniture (and computer) and then lay new carpet when I got a phone call. When I answered it, I was a bit disoriented — the carpet glue was going to my head (!), but I recognized the voice immediately. It was Berthold from Westhorpe University, and he was wondering if I would be willing to come out to Vermont and to work with them, even on a temporary basis. Can you believe it? I was overjoyed!

It was doubly weird because I was sitting at my computer, and what did I have in my hand? I had a Vermont Life desk calendar and I was flipping through the photos, idly thinking about life and kicking myself for having given up the Westhorpe University opportunity.

Of course, you know as well as I do that it was impossible for me to take it. After Marshall's car accident, he had the incident with his dad. His dad took the car Marshall had bought with everything he could save, borrow, or sell. I realize that Marshall's dad did contribute some money, but it was just really weird that he refused to acknowledge any contribution of Marshall's. He acted as though HE had put in all the money. That was such a delusion! In point of fact, Marshall contributed almost all the money. That reminded me so much of what it was like to live with him. Arrgh. I wonder how long his present wife will be able to endure it.

And, as things worked out, it was definitely for the best. Marshall is living with me now, and he's doing well in school. He likes the job he got where he works twice a week for a few hours at the Wet Seal, a clothing store at the mall. He's working with people he knows from school, so that helps. He feels quite successful and good about himself. Plus, he's starting to recover his strength (although he's still dreadfully thin). Perhaps the nicest moment was when he wrote a chapter in his Autobiography (a project for his English class) entitled "My Mom." Then, on Mother's Day, he gave me 16 ivory roses — one for each year I had been a mom. It was so sweet — I could hardly believe it.

It's great that Westhorpe is still interested. I'll go in August, just when I had already applied (and received approval) for vacation.

It will give me a chance to think about what it means to be an "ethnic Vermonter" from a family that has been in Vermont since 1762. It will give me a chance to think about roots, and the origin of attitudes and values. Vermonters are known for their creativity (eccentricity), independent attitudes, freethinking, and emphasis on family. I know I connect on some deep spiritual level. Perhaps that is why I've had the experience I've had with guys. I like guys and I like having men friends, but I like the weird ones (!). These things don't always work out. Oh well.

So, I'm going to buy a ticket. While I'm up there, I think I'll drive around, see the sites, think about things. It will be very positive. Perhaps I'll start learning how to look at things in a different way instead of feeling overwhelmed, defensive, and perversely disgruntled about life.

Well, that's probably asking too much.

Do you think you'd like to go with me?

Love,
Susan

1 August
Montpelier, Vermont

Tek:

I'm in Montpelier, Vermont, and I'm in the New England Culinary Institute's restaurant, La Brioche. It's very pleasant — scrupulously clean, cheerful, with fresh hot coffee, fresh breads, nice pastries, vegetable dishes, and fruits. The manager is a Hungarian woman. She is taking a break, and is seated at a table with two other women. One is European, the other is American. They are discussing the differences between American and European women.

They conclude, after a long discussion, that American women have some advantages because there seems to be less prejudice toward women. "Oh, but that depends upon where you are!" says the American. "Women in the southern part of the US are not treated well in large organizations. The difference in pay is huge."

I was not a part of the discussion, but I agreed.

"In the US, many women own small businesses. They can have economic freedom," they continued.

But, they also concluded that European women have a deeper sense of family commitment, particularly to the aging members of their families. European women see themselves as a part of a family system. American women try to extricate themselves from their families, which are often viewed as restrictive or abusive.

The view that American women are aggressive, direct, and loudmouthed was expressed. Cool. I had the idea that they thought American women were tough, and they took no abuse from anyone, ever.

Wouldn't that be nice! If it were only true! Then I wouldn't have to write so many letters in which I present a version of life I only wish were true. I write about the things I wish I had done, the things I wish I had said. The truth is, I sit, I observe, I conform in silence, and then I either stay or run away. Why fight when you can run?

Oh well.

Vermont encourages these open dialogues, with no penalties for opinions expressed.

My personal opinion is that all women have difficult lives. All women have many roles and responsibilities, and not as many options as might be ideal. Men have difficulties, too, of course.

It's a beautiful day, bright green mountains, crystal-clear springs and lakes. Montpelier has become a center for handmade crafts, handwoven sweaters, lovely carved furniture, and handmade candles and glassware.

I think I'll buy some earrings at Cool Jewels down the street.

Love,
Susan

4 August
Island Pond, Vermont
after an afternoon's wandering in Quebec

D:

I don't know how it happened, but before I knew it, the stop signs said "Arret" instead of "Stop" and the speed limits became impossibly high for these curving roads — 50? — and then I realized it meant 50 km per hour, not 50 miles per hour, and that I must be in Canada — Quebec, to be exact. Inever crossed any sort of border guard or checkpoint — I just wandered down the rocky dirt road that seemed to go from farm to farm, parallel to the US / Canada border.

It's amazing, though. Within a few miles, you can tell that this is not Vermont. It doesn't look at all like woodsy, rocky Vermont. Quebec is a series of large rolling meadows and giant dairy operations. It seems quite prosperous, except there are people. The Quebec-style farm is very distinctive — red-roofed barns and houses, some in whimsical shapes — octagonal or round.

The towns were settled at approximately the same time as Vermont towns. I determined this as the winding road took me to Dixville and then to Coaticook, est. 1782. There must have been some serious competition going on at the time between France, the newly liberated colonies, and England. I suppose the French won here. This is thoroughly French, and I don't think that people actually speak much English, just as the Americans across the border do not speak French, unless they are of French descent.

This border is ridiculously porous. I should be as French-Canadian as possible. I turned to a French-Canadian public radio channel. I can understand about 40 percent of it — enough to realize that they are discussing the work of a Mexican choreographer from Hermosillo, and they are focusing in on the impact of his homosexuality on his life, his work, his art. In truth, I understood it only fragmentarily, but it seemed like a good idea to try to attune my ear to French just in case I had to buy gas, order food, or ask for directions.

Unfortunately, most of the vocabulary in this radio program is more or less useless for such tasks — homosexuality, isolation, exigency, suffer, art, dance corps, guilt, mother. I'm trying desperately to remember all the helpful phrases I learned in my French classes at the university. They are similarly useless terms and phrases, primarily used in literary analysis. Oh well.

Where is my courage? Where is my sense of adventure? Where is that brazen, shameless Susan who will go anywhere, do anything, try any language? Maybe she finally learned a thing or two.

Just as I was making yet another wrong turn, I happen across an incredibly beautiful lake, utterly deserted (it had just stopped raining), with a staggering, breathtaking view of "Le Mont Pinacle," a large hunk of rock which juts up on one side. It appears to be some sort of volcanic or metamorphic rock, jointed and dark. Surrounding the bare rock face are trees, and the absolutely pristine surface of the water. There are no boats on the lake. I drive further and run into a lovely little golf course. There are two or three golfers. There is also a sign: *Vendre.* I wonder what it would be like to buy a lake house in this remote yet unspeakably gorgeous place. I might try to find this place again next weekend.

In Coaticook, a guy seated on his front porch is laughing at me as I drive over a curb as I exit the parking lot of a little restaurant. I smile and laugh, too. I wonder what he's like. Does he have a sense of humor? What does he like to talk about? Where does he work? Does he like sex? What? Okay. Something is definitely wrong with me. I need to pull my head together. Something is definitely not well in the old *gulliva* — and ... why am I mixing Russian with French words?

Hmm. I have next weekend off, too. Perhaps I can sneak across the border again and go to a larger town and see what kind of jobs are available. Of course, I don't really speak French... *tres problematique* ... and, why would I have to sneak across the border? It is not illegal for Americans to visit

Canada. Ah, but yes, I have a rental car! I think it's not cool to drive a rental car across a border. I know it's not okay to do it in Mexico. Maybe it's different up here. And then I could check into a cute little hotel, find a club, dance all night to techno music, and then have sex until the sun comes up ... what? I am really very unbalanced. There must be something in the air. These are ridiculous thoughts. But it is so beautiful, and I feel so relaxed and content.

I was not able to sneak back across the border the same way I sneaked in. The US border official was deeply intrigued by my passport.

"You've been in Kazakhstan? Where do you live?" he asked. I explained I live in Oklahoma, and am just driving around, visiting. My car has Connecticut license tags. I'm sure that seemed weird. I wonder if he thought that I might be some sort of weird American in the employ of a Russian group that smuggles Chinese guys and kidnaps or tricks Ukrainian girls across the border for sweatshops and prostitution rings in the US? My hair is bleached. Do I look fake? Do I seem Russian?

Russian? That is pretty impossible. I explained to him that I have relatives in Bloomfield.

"Well, you took a wrong turn at Island Pond," he said. He looked at my passport again.

He hands me back my passport and wishes me well. On the way back to Island Pond, there is a minor traffic jam. A moose is walking along the side of the road. It is not clear if it will dart into traffic or run back into the woods. This is definitely the best time to be here. Last year I was here in November. The woods were grim, gray and cold. I don't like the dark and the cold. I like it that the sun rises at 5 a.m. and sets at 10 p.m..

I'm glad I'm here. This all makes sense now. Everything is coming together.

And, someday I'll be able to even explain to you how and why. I miss you more than you might imagine.

All best,
S

RE: DISREGARD "YOU'RE IN BIG TROUBLE"

5 August
Williamstown, Vermont

Dear Marshall:

I am so sorry — you have every right to be very annoyed with me for sending you an e-mail threatening you with "big trouble" for not sending me the daily e-mail to let me know you're okay while you're "minding the house" while I'm here in Vermont. I mean — you obviously had sent the e-mail messages, I just didn't see them right away in the cluttered forest of junk correspondence — horoscopes, lucky numbers, special prize offers, joblists, vacation offers, etc.. So I panicked.

You're right — I shouldn't jump to conclusions. In my defense, I am simply following the example of President Bush, who was accused by a news commentator of always "leaping before he looks."

Okay. That's no excuse.

And, I'm really proud of you for being able to take care of things. But, if anything happened to you, I would never forgive myself! And, be nice to Grandmother and Granddad — and don't complain so much when Grandmother tells you to eat vegetables. She did that when I was a kid, too. Remember, there are a lot of people there if you need anything — Grandmother and Granddad, Aunt Tek, Uncle Todd, and (if you're really desperate), your dad.

Yesterday evening, there was a discussion in the kitchen of this little Vermont country inn where I'm staying. Some guy from California (although born in Mexico) who drove up in his Lexus for a "business development executive" position with a web-design company was talking about how his mom raised him all by herself. Then the owner of the inn started talking about how she raised nine kids by herself.

They both said the key was being a tough mom and having a firm and rigid discipline system. They asked me about my experience. I told them that I had come to the conclusion that I had made a mistake by thinking that I had to be hyper-vigilant, and that the "team discipline" with his dad had just turned into something that resembled two paranoid prison guards just waiting to set the dogs on the prisoner.

"I decided my son needed an advocate, and that was what I needed to be," I said.

There was a shocked silence.

Then the woman who owns the inn said, "You know, if you're an advocate, then all you are doing is protecting your child from the consequences of his actions."

"You mean, like the time he downloaded from the Internet instructions on how to make bombs and explosives, including napalm?" That was my attempt at humor.

They both turned to me with grim, stone-faced expressions.

"My God! If my mom had ever caught me doing that on the Internet, she would have taken my computer away from me forever! My friends and I skateboarded on the cul-de-sac," said the guy from California. He had shaved his head to disguise the fact that he was bald in the middle. I tried to guess how old he was. He acted around 40, but I think he was about 26.

"Where is your son now?" they both asked.

"He's staying at home. Grandparents." I hoped they would jump to the conclusion that you were staying with Grandmother and Granddad.

They made some more comments about how bad and deviant kids are today (as though they weren't before) and how single moms today let them run wild (as though a mother with a dozen kids and no electricity, gas, or running water could pay much attention to the kids). I hung around to seem polite, then escaped as quickly as I could.

I had lots of bad dreams.

So, please accept my apologies (if you can) for being so panicky and for accusing you of things you did not do. I will try to improve. You deserve to have a mom who at least listens to you, is patient, and tries to find out all the facts before threatening you with punishments, or throwing in the towel, throwing up my hands, giving up, whatever...

The truth is, I'm really proud of you, and you are much more mature than I was at your age. I'm very impressed at your ability to do well at work, your clear head about school and friends, and your compassionate approach to animals — for example, the cat who had kittens in the air conditioner next door. A lot of teenagers would have turned on the air conditioner just to see what the cats would do.

Take care of yourself, drive carefully, be safe and enjoy yourself.

Love from
MOM

ON WILLIAM'S "GAME ROOM"

9 August
Williamstown, Vermont
after visiting the great "Northeast Kingdom" again

Hi Tek:

I was reading in today's paper that Europeans just do not understand Americans' fascination with guns, religion, and the death penalty.

After going up to Bloomfield, and then to camp, and seeing our cousins William, Alex, and Uncle Roth, I had the feeling that Europeans would find our family to be pragmatically American, pragmatically weird.

I agree. We are weird. Not that knowledge means power to change (unfortunately).

I got a chance to visit William's Game Room. It gave me a good taste of another American obsession — hunting. The Game Room was filled with wild game found within a three mile radius of his house. There were bears, deer, moose, minks, raccoons, ermine, wildcats, chipmunks, and more — all sent to a taxidermist, stuffed, and mounted on the wall. It was like going to a museum of natural history. Apparently, hunters and tourists love to stop in. They buy maple syrup, and then they look at the "game." It was absolutely macabre, but I don't think William saw it that way.

He even had a few framed poems on the wall — song lyrics, he said.

I saw the moose and he saw me —
I heard the words he tried to say —
Take me, William, Take me —
And I knew it had to be that way
Because we were the same — him and me —
wanting the fastest track to immortality.

"Immortality?" I asked. "The moose dies, gets its head mounted on the wall, and it's immortality for you and for him?"

"Yeah. That's it," said William.

"Couldn't you just take its photograph and put it on the wall?" I asked.

"No. It wouldn't be the same," he said.

Then he showed me the commendation he had gotten from the governor of the State of Vermont. Apparently, a guy in New Hampshire, just north of here had been angry with the government. He had been a member of Special Forces —

but I guess he just snapped. I will say that he seemed to use his training for all the wrong purposes. He built explosive devices with the plan to blow up a dam. Then he went on a killing rampage. The madman killed a policeman, then stole his car. Then he killed some government employees, then drove to Bloomfield, where he promptly ran into a tree in front of the house that William was painting. That was after the madman had shot a game warden who staggered out of his truck and fell down the river bank.

William rescued him, even though the madman had gotten out of his stolen police car and was hunting them as though they were deer (or moose). Apparently, he thought that William's paintbrush was some sort of new kind of gun, and he turned around and left (instead of shooting William, who was dragging the game warden up the bank to take him to the hospital).

The madman was eventually caught in Brunswick Springs. He was shot dead by the Vermont State Police. Apparently he had enough fertilizer bombs to blow up the dam, plus three buildings the size of the federal building in Oklahoma City. What drove him mad? We'll never know. He was shot dead as he tried to kill another police officer.

As William was telling me this, and showing me the commendation medal, Alex came by. He was surprised to see me, too. He mentioned that his store was prospering. Then, the story came out about how he had the opportunity to buy the place. The owner was a friend of William. He had started to dabble in drugs, and his girlfriend had the same problem. No one knew how bad the problem had gotten until William went to visit him, and found that he had blown his head off with his deer rifle. Apparently, he and his girlfriend had a suicide pact. But, she chose not to follow. But, then, three months later, she, too, committed suicide. The store came up for sale.

What a grim place. It is beautiful, but the physical beauty does not seem to have an impact on people's lives. I don't really understand it — nature is supposed to have a calming, soothing effect.

Instead, it seems to encourage all that "Wild West" mentality — barbarous violence, hunting, guns, extremist stances towards law and religion — that mentality that Europeans find so inexplicable.

I have to say I find it inexplicable, too.

Now. Where can I buy a moose rifle? (hah hah).

Love,
Susan

15 August
Williamstown, Vermont

D:

This is the letter I never thought I'd send you. It's the one where I let you know I have to stop writing to you.

Is it because you've offended me? No.

Is it because I couldn't control my mind and I'm angry with you because thinking of you makes me sad? No.

You mean to me more than I can ever express. I love you. I have always loved you. It has been hard living with the realization that I never did tell you, though. When I had the chance, I just sat around with you, yammering on about supposedly intellectual topics. What were we really talking about, though? Tabloids, scandals, and self-doubt.

That's why I loved you so much. Too bad I could never muster the courage to say it.

After spending the last year or so lost in a web of tangled feelings, desires, and self-doubt, one thing has become clear. The path will never be clear.

Perhaps that's the great lesson in all of this contemplation — I'll always be lost, bitchy, whiny, and frustrated. Hmm. So much for a "path to enlightenment."

But you've helped me more than you know. You've helped me work out my thoughts about Marshall, you've helped me see my relationship with my past and with my family (especially my sister and my father). You've also given me permission to say the things I can't really express when I'm with other people.

It is 2001. This year will mark 10 years since we met. It will mark five years since we last saw each other. I still am very sad about what happened, and I will visit you in Elko. I'm not sure how or where to find you. I suppose there are directories for those sorts of places.

Did you know my dad was president and chief executive officer of a small mining company headquartered in Elko? He bought it in 1970, then he and his partner sold it in 1982 when gold prices were at their highest. His partner is gone. He's someplace in Elko. I may look him up. But maybe not. He was never the friend to me that you have been.

I'm getting ready to go back to Oklahoma. I know I'll be coming here to Vermont more often now, and I'll bring Marshall with me.

Thank you for everything you have done — thank you for listening. I only wish I had been able to tell you my feelings about things. Too bad I didn't. But, maybe it wasn't necessary. You knew, didn't you?

This marks some sort of recovery. I can just hear you telling me that. It's a turning point. It's a step in the right direction. Writing to a blank screen & hitting "send" as though this e-mail would go anywhere except into cyber-ether is crazy. Or is it? I needed to talk to someone. I needed to tell someone the truth. Why couldn't it be you? Yes, you. You offered yourself up, just like you did in the past. We were always so compatible, except when it mattered. Isn't that one of life's little ironies (!).

Now I'll lay the flowers on the side of the road somewhere since I don't know where you're buried and wonder why it was you and not me.

Always, with love,
S

Photo by Catherine Kerley

SINCE HER TEENAGE YEARS, Susan has been on an endless road trip of the mind, in a kind of "Endless Summer" travel, searching for the perfect wave, the wildest mountain, the most vivid sunset-sunrise sequence, the most expressive language for poetry, literature, geology—and since the mid-90s, the Internet. In her quest for intellectual and emotional "limit experiences," Susan has learned various languages (some well, others for survival) and has traveled throughout South and Central America, much of Central Asia, the Caucasus, Russia, Africa, and Europe. Her Ph.D. dissertation on apocalyptic narratives dealt with cultural studies, film, and literary texts. Since receiving her Ph.D. in 1996, Susan has focused on education and economic development and has developed onsite and web-based educational programs for entities in Paraguay, Colombia, Uzbekistan, and Azerbaijan, as well as the online courses and programs she has developed and overseen for universities and textbook publishers in the US. Susan is the recipient of awards and grants for her work with Paraguayan women writers (PEN award, Oklahoma Book Award finalist, Paraguayan-American Cultural Center commendation), for promoting Slovenian writers, and for her poetry and experimental writing (Gertrude Stein Award, Oklahoma Book Award, Trubar Award, and others). Susan lives in Norman, Oklahoma, where she is director of online curriculum development for the University of Oklahoma, and is chair of the Institute for Stabilization through Technology. Her son, Michael, is a US Marine.